D0281103
ROLLER GIRL

UGH, THERE'S ONLY ASTRID HERE. I TOLD YOU, ONLY BABIES HANG OUT AT THE PARK.
COME ON, LET'S GO TO THE MALL. I DON'T KNOW WHY YOU WANTED TO COME HERE ANYWAY.
CLICK

ROLLER GIRL
PUFFIN
by Victoria Jamieson

BETTER CALL MALL SECURITY, YOU JERKS!
PRETZEL KING
AAAAAAAAGH!
OMG, I CHIPPED A NAIL!

PUFFIN BOOKS

UK | USA | CANADA | IRELAND | AUSTRALIA
INDIA | NEW ZEALAND | SOUTH AFRICA

PUFFIN BOOKS IS PART OF THE PENGUIN RANDOM HOUSE GROUP OF COMPANIES
WHOSE ADDRESSES CAN BE FOUND AT GLOBAL.PENGUINRANDOMHOUSE.COM.

WWW.PENGUIN.CO.UK WWW.PUFFIN.CO.UK WWW.LADYBIRD.CO.UK

FIRST PUBLISHED IN THE USA BY DIAL BOOKS 2015
PUBLISHED BY ARRANGEMENT WITH PENGUIN YOUNG READERS GROUP,
A DIVISION OF PENGUIN RANDOM HOUSE LLC
PUBLISHED IN GREAT BRITAIN BY PUFFIN BOOKS 2017

003

DESIGNED BY VICTORIA JAMIESON AND JASON HENRY

THE ARTWORK FOR THIS BOOK WAS CREATED WITH INK AND COLOURED DIGITALLY

PRINTED IN CHINA

A CIP CATALOGUE RECORD FOR THIS BOOK IS
AVAILABLE FROM THE BRITISH LIBRARY

ISBN: 978-0-141-37899-2

ALL CORRESPONDENCE TO:
PUFFIN BOOKS, PENGUIN RANDOM HOUSE CHILDREN'S
80 STRAND, LONDON WC2R ORL

Penguin Random House is committed to a sustainable future for our business, our readers and our planet. This book is made from Forest Stewardship Council® certified paper.

Many thanks to skaters around the world who let me borrow their derby names for some of my characters. This book is dedicated to them, and to all the skaters, officials, volunteers, and fans who bring roller derby to life. I'm so proud to be part of this incredible community.

CHAPTER 1
How it all began
IF YOU REALLY WANT TO KNOW, IT ALL BEGAN BACK IN FIFTH GRADE. BACK WHEN NICOLE AND I WERE STILL BEST FRIENDS.
OK, YOU TWO. IN THE CAR.
C'MON, MOM, CAN'T YOU TELL US WHERE WE'RE GOING?
NOPE, IT'S A SURPRISE.
THEN MOM UTTERED THE WORDS THAT NEVER FAILED TO STRIKE FEAR AND DREAD INTO MY HEART...
...TONIGHT, WE ARE HAVING AN EVENING OF CULTURAL ENLIGHTENMENT!
ou girls are going to love this!
strong, positive female role model
You are so lucky.
When I was your age...
THIS DID NOT BODE WELL FOR OUR FRIDAY NIGHT. WE'D EXPERIENCED ONE OR TWO OF MOM'S **ECE**S BEFORE.

POETRY READINGS...
HA
HA
HA
THE OPERA...
AND THE MODERN ART GALLERY, TO NAME A FEW. AND THOSE WERE THE **GOOD** TRIPS.
?
?
!

ON THE OTHER HAND, MAYBE TONIGHT WAS STARTING TO SHAPE UP.

OAKS
AMUSEMENT PARK
HEY, ARE WE GOING TO THE AMUSEMENT PARK?
NOT EXACTLY...
WE GOT IN A LONG LINE OF STRANGE-LOOKING PEOPLE.
MOM
MOM, ARE YOU SELLING US TO THE CIRCUS?
MRS. V., I'M TOO YOUNG TO BE A LION-TAMER!
KEEP IT UP, YOU TWO.

I WANT TO BE THE TATTOOED LADY.
NO WAY—**I** WANT TO BE THE TATTOOED LADY! YOU CAN BE THE BEARDED LADY.
TICKETS, PLEASE.
WE WENT IN THIS HUGE BUILDING THAT LOOKED LIKE AN AIRPLANE HANGAR.
MOM, CAN I GET A TATTOO?
I WANT TO DYE MY HAIR PINK!
CAN I GET A NOSE RING?
CAN I GET A LIP RING?

JUST AS WE SAT DOWN IN THE BLEACHERS...
HEY, WHAT **IS** THIS PLACE?

...THE LIGHTS WENT OUT.

Clap Clap Clap
Whoo
Clap
Clap Clap
Clap
ooo
YEAH!
oo!!
Clap
Clap
LADIES AND GENTLEMEN...
ARE YOU READY FOR SOME...

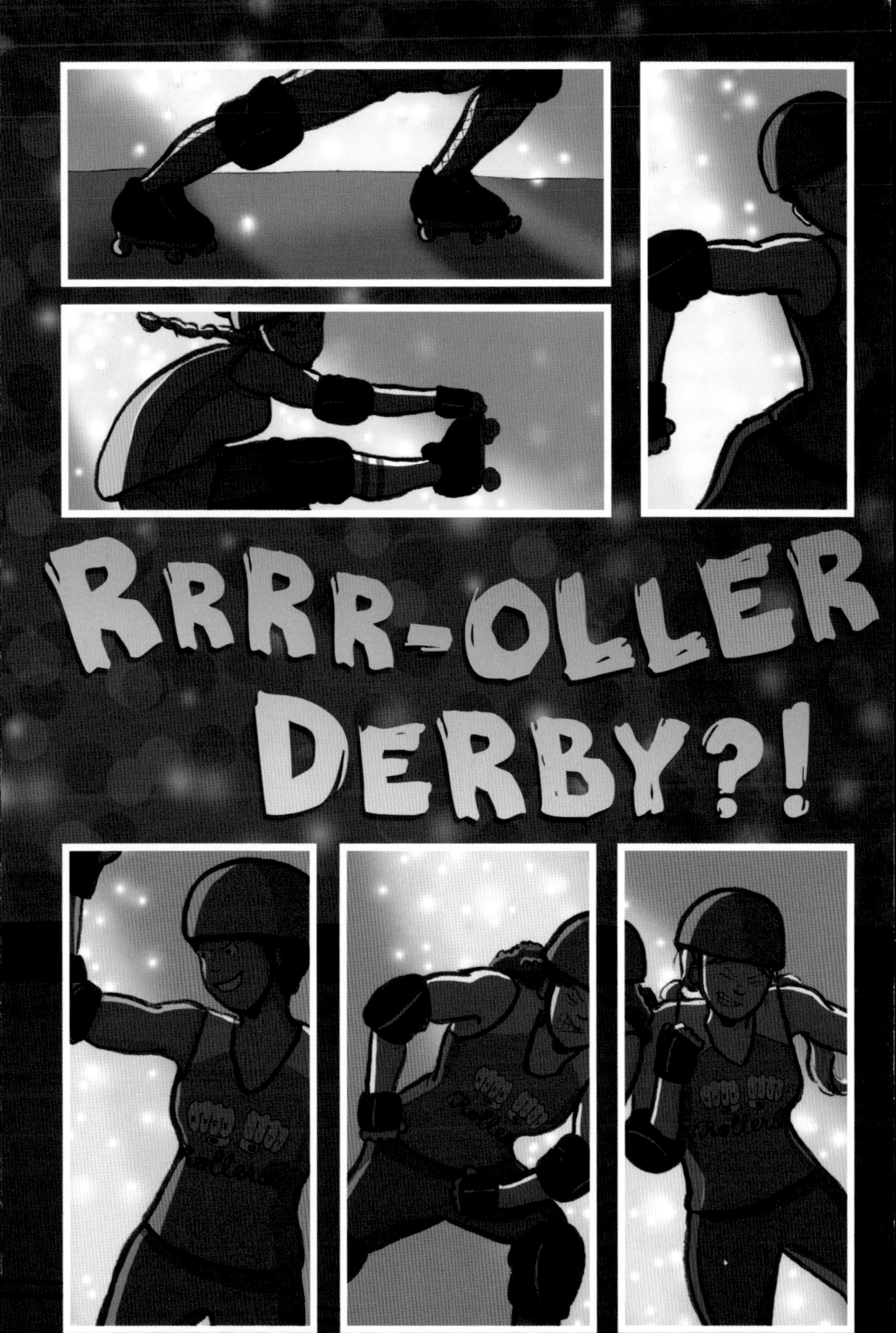
RRRR-OLLER
DERBY?!

INTRODUCING YOUR TWO TEAMS... PLEASE WELCOME OUR VISITING SKATERS, THE OREGON CITY ROLLERGIRLS!
AND OF COURSE, PORTLAND'S HOMETOWN HEROES... THE ROSE CITY ROLLERS!
WHATEVER THIS IS... IT'S A LOT BETTER THAN THE ART MUSEUM!
SEE? YOUR OLD MOM IS ALL RIGHT FROM TIME TO TIME.
ROLLER DERBY

THE EMCEE ANNOUNCED THE PLAYERS, AND THEY ALL HAD CRAZY NAMES LIKE...
SCALD EAGLE
THE BLAST UNICORN
YOGA NABI SARI
SCRAPPY GO LUCKY
ROARSHOCK TESS
THEY ALL LOOKED REALLY TOUGH— SORT OF LIKE THE INMATES IN THAT DOCUMENTARY ABOUT WOMEN'S PRISONS MOM MADE ME WATCH A FEW ECES AGO.
WEIRD HAIR
TATTOOS
STRANGE OUTFITS
CREEPY MAKEUP

THEN THE PLAYERS LINED UP, THE REFS BLEW A WHISTLE... AND THEY WERE OFF!
TWEET!
AT FIRST I COULDN'T TELL WHAT WAS GOING ON—JUST A BUNCH OF SKATING, HITTING, AND FALLING.

MOM, LEMME SEE YOUR PROGRAM!
. . . "PLEASE."
I CAN'T WATCH!
MOM'S PROGRAM EXPLAINED SOME OF THE RULES.
BASICALLY THERE IS THIS jammer, WHO WEARS A STAR ON HER HELMET.
SHE TRIES TO PASS THE blockers ON THE OTHER TEAM. FOR EVERY BLOCKER SHE PASSES, SHE GETS A POINT.
1 + 1 + 1 + 1 = 4 points
OF COURSE, THE BLOCKERS DON'T WANT HER TO SCORE POINTS. THAT'S WHERE ALL THE HITTING AND FALLING COMES IN.
TAKE THAT, SPEEDY!

THERE WAS THIS ONE JAMMER, RAINBOW BITE. YOU COULD ALWAYS TELL WHO SHE WAS BECAUSE SHE WORE RAINBOW SOCKS.
ROSE CITY Rollers
SHE LOOKED LIKE A SUPERHERO.
ISN'T THIS THE BEST THING YOU'VE EVER SEEN?
WELL, IT'S A LITTLE... SCARY.
GEEZ, NICOLE... YOU CAN BE SUCH A *BABY* SOMETIMES.

AT HALFTIME WE ASKED MOM IF WE COULD GO SIT ON THE FLOOR BY OURSELVES... AND SHE SAID YES!
MAYBE WE'LL SIT NEXT TO SOME CUTE BOYS!
YOU'RE KINDA MISSING THE POINT, NICOLE.
AWESOME.
THIS IS HOW CLOSE WE WERE TO THE ACTION:
SKATERS
US*
FOAM BARRIER
*NOTE THAT NICOLE IS *HAPPY* IN THIS DRAWING. THIS IS KNOWN AS "ARTISTIC LICENSE."
SEE, THEY'RE LAUGHING AND HAVING FUN... IT'S A **GAME**!
I GUESS SO...

LADIES AND GENTLEMEN, AS WE START THE SECOND HALF, WE'VE GOT RAINBOW BITE ON THE JAMMER LINE. SHE'S UP AGAINST ILLEGALLY BLONDE, AND THESE TWO ARE **FIERCE** COMPETITORS!
OOH, AND RAINBOW BITE TAKES A **BIG** HIT IN TURN TWO!
Gasp!
Gasp!
Gasp!
Gasp! Gasp! Gasp!

WINK

AND WITH A WINK AND A SMILE, SHE'S BACK ON HER SKATES AND BACK IN THE GAME! AND THAT, LADIES AND GENTLEMEN, IS WHAT I CALL . . .

. . . A TRUE CHAMPION!

AND THEN, BEFORE I KNEW IT...THE GAME WAS OVER!
C'MON, IT'S TIME TO GO, WEIRDO!
MOM EVEN LET US GET T-SHIRTS FROM THE GIFT SHOP!
PINK!
BLACK!
THIS WAS A REAL MIRACLE, BECAUSE MOM USUALLY AVOIDS GIFT SHOPS LIKE THE PLAGUE.
MUSEUM OF SCIENCE & INDUSTRY
FIVE DOLLARS FOR A PENCIL?!? YOU'VE GOT TO BE KIDDING ME!
AND HERE, SOMETHING SPECIAL FOR YOU LADIES. ON THE HOUSE!
WHOA! A POSTER OF RAINBOW BITE!
ROLLER DERBY
WHY DON'T YOU ASK HER TO SIGN IT? LOOK, SHE'S RIGHT OVER THERE!
WHAT?! NO! I CAN'T!
AACK! NO! NO WAY!

THEN, ON THE WAY HOME WE STOPPED AT BURGERTOWN! WHO WAS THIS WOMAN, AND WHAT DID SHE DO WITH MY MOTHER?
BURGERTOWN
BURGERTOWN
TRY OUR ONION RINGS
I SHOULD HAVE ASKED RAINBOW BITE TO SIGN MY POSTER. WHY DIDN'T I ASK HER TO SIGN MY POSTER?
DID YOU SEE HOW FAST SHE WAS? SHE WAS LIKE, SO FAST!
DID YOU SEE WHEN SHE FELL RIGHT IN FRONT OF US?
THANK YOU.
I'LL JUST HAVE A SALAD, PLEASE.
THAT'S ALL YOU WANT?
MY MOM SAID I SHOULD START WATCHING WHAT I EAT.
AND THEN RAINBOW BITE WINKED AT *ME*. RIGHT AT **ME**!

BY THE WAY, DID YOU SEE THIS IN THE PROGRAM? THERE'S A JUNIOR ROLLER DERBY CAMP, STARTING THIS SUMMER.
ROLLER DERBY
WHAT?! LET ME SEE! PLEASE!
Mo's Burgers
Portland!
IT STARTS NEXT MONTH, RIGHT AFTER SCHOOL LETS OUT.
City Rosebuds
Roller Derby League
JUNIOR ROLLER DERBY CAMP!
Open to Girls Ages 12-17
Skate!
Make friends!
Have fun!
June 23- July 25
Register today!
PDX
ROSEBUDS

AND JUST LIKE THAT, MY FATE WAS DECIDED.

I WAS GOING TO BE A ROLLER GIRL.

CHAPTER 2
ROLLER DERBY
BRIGHT AND EARLY THE NEXT MORNING, IT WAS TIME TO START ON MY NEW LIFE.
FIRST, I HUNG MY NEW POSTER RIGHT OVER MY BED. IT WAS ABOUT TIME I COVERED UP THAT OLD SOLAR SYSTEM MURAL ANYWAY. I'VE ONLY BEEN LOOKING AT IT SINCE SECOND GRADE.
NOW RAINBOW BITE WOULD BE THE FIRST THING I SAW IN THE MORNING, AND THE LAST THING I SAW AT NIGHT.
NEXT, I MADE A LIST USING EVERYTHING I KNEW FROM WATCHING SPORTS MOVIES.
1) Roller skate!!
!!!!!!!!!!!!!!!!!!!
2) Lift weights
3) Eat raw eggs
4) watch more sports movies

NUMBER ONE ON THE LIST SEEMED THE MOST APPEALING, SO I DECIDED TO START THERE.
GOOD MORNING, DEAR MOTHER. WOULD YOU CARE FOR SOME FRESH-SQUEEZED ORANGE JUICE?
YOUR HAIR LOOKS LOVELY IN THIS FLUORESCENT LIGHTING. ARE YOU DOING SOMETHING NEW WITH IT?
WHAT DO YOU WANT?
CAN YOU TAKE ME AND NICOLE TO THE ROLLER SKATING RINK? PLEASE? PLEASE? *PLEASE*?!
SIGH WHAT HAVE I CREATED? OK, GET SOME CLOTHES ON AND WE'LL LEAVE IN AN HOUR.
ONE STEP AHEAD OF YOU, MOM!
DROP
DO YOU KNOW IF NICOLE EVEN WANTS TO COME?
OH, SHE'LL WANT TO COME, I KNOW SHE WILL.
OF COURSE SHE'D WANT TO COME. WE WERE BEST FRIENDS, AND THAT'S WHAT BEST FRIENDS DO. THEY DO EVERYTHING TOGETHER.

MAYBE YOU'RE WONDERING BY NOW HOW NICOLE AND I BECAME BEST FRIENDS IN THE FIRST PLACE.
ACTUALLY, IT WAS THANKS TO KNOW-IT-ALL RACHEL. AND THE DEAD SQUIRREL.
RACHEL WAS A BOSSY JERK, EVEN BACK IN FIRST GRADE.
NOBODY TOUCH THAT SQUIRREL.
SHE RUBBED ME THE WRONG WAY RIGHT FROM THE START.
YOU'RE NOT THE BOSS OF EVERYONE.
I *SAID*, DON'T TOUCH IT!
YOU CAN'T TELL ME WHAT TO DO.

TOUCH
RABIES! ASTRID HAS RABIES!
I DO NOT!
STAY AWAY FROM HER— YOU MIGHT CATCH IT.
NOW YOU'RE GOING TO START FOAMING AT THE MOUTH, AND THEN YOU'LL GO CRAZY, AND THEN YOU'LL **DIE**.

WHEN I GOT BACK INSIDE, I ASKED MISS JUDKINS IF I COULD USE THE BATHROOM.
ARE YOU FEELING ALL RIGHT? YOU DON'T LOOK SO WELL.
RABIES!
I WASHED MY HANDS ABOUT 50 TIMES IN HOT WATER.
WAS I FOAMING AT THE MOUTH? OR WERE THOSE JUST SPIT BUBBLES?
I REALLY WASN'T FEELING WELL AT ALL. MAYBE I DID HAVE RABIES. MAYBE THIS WAS THE END.
WHY DID I TOUCH IT? WHY?

BUT THEN...
HELLO?
...NICOLE CAME IN WITH THE OTHER HALL PASS.
LET ME SEE YOUR HANDS.
YOU DON'T HAVE ANY CUTS ON YOUR HANDS...YOU'LL BE FINE.
ARE YOU SURE? *SNIFF*
OH, YES. MY AUNT IS A DOCTOR, AND SHE TELLS ME THESE THINGS.
AND JUST LIKE THAT, I FELT BETTER RIGHT AWAY.

NICOLE STAYED WITH ME WHILE I WASHED MY HANDS ONE MORE TIME.
SHE HANDED ME A BIG STACK OF PAPER TOWELS WHEN I WAS DONE.
WHEN SOMEONE SAVES YOUR LIFE LIKE THAT...
EXIT
...YOU CAN'T HELP BUT BECOME BEST FRIENDS.

CHAPTER 3
BUT BACK TO NOW. AND ROLLER SKATING. NICOLE *DID* WANT TO COME, JUST LIKE I SAID SHE WOULD.
SKATE WORLD
I'M GOING TO BE, LIKE, THE TIGER WOODS OF ROLLER SKATING.
WELL, I'LL BE THE MICHELLE KWAN, WHICH IS EVEN BETTER BECAUSE SHE'S ACTUALLY A SKATER.
REMEMBER, NICOLE'S MOM WILL PICK YOU UP AT 11, AND SHE'LL TAKE YOU HOME AFTER NICOLE'S BALLET CLASS. CALL IF YOU NEED ANYTHING. STICK TOGETHER.
'KAY. BYE, MOM.
HEY, THERE'S ADAM AND KEITH!
I COULD BARELY WAIT TO START SKATING.
MY MOM GAVE ME $20. MAYBE WE CAN GO TO THE SNACK BAR LATER.
UH-HUH.
MAYBE RAINBOW BITE WOULD BE PRACTICING HERE TODAY. MAYBE ROLLER DERBY TEAMS MADE EXCEPTIONS FOR VERY TALENTED YOUNG SKATERS.

WHOA, LOOK AT HER GO!
SHE'S SO FAST!
BACKWARD TOO?
WHAT?!
IT TOOK ME MONTHS TO LEARN THAT TRICK!
FLIP
THAT DOES IT, WE HAVE TO HAVE HER ON OUR TEAM.
COME ON!
COMING!
IT'S HARD TO SKATE ON THIS CARPET.
THIS WAS IT. I WAS ONE STEP AWAY FROM REALIZING MY DESTINY.

STEP
THUNK
HOW
DO YOU
STAND
UP?
YOU JUST SORT OF... BEND YOUR KNEES AND PUSH TO THE SIDE.
I **AM** BENDING MY KNEES.

NICOLE SKATED NEXT TO ME WHILE I CLUNG TO THE WALL.
THAT'S IT! YOU'RE LOOKING BETTER!
LOOK, THIS MUST BE BORING FOR YOU. WHY DON'T YOU SKATE AROUND SOME?
WELL . . . OK.
I WATCHED AS SHE SKATED FASTER AND FASTER. HOW DID SHE KNOW HOW TO DO THIS?
I WATCHED AS SHE . . .
SKATED OVER TO ADAM BISHOP?!

OOF!
PLEASE DON'T HANG ON TO THE WALL LIKE THAT. YOU'RE IN MY LITTLE BOY'S WAY.
YOU NEED TO BE MORE CAREFUL— THERE ARE LOTS OF LITTLE KIDS HERE.
NO KIDDING.
I MADE IT TO THE EXIT EVENTUALLY...
DON'T ASK ME HOW.

IN FACT, I MADE IT ALL THE WAY TO A BATHROOM STALL, WHERE I PLANNED TO SPEND THE NEXT HOUR.
STORY OF MY LIFE.
HELLO?
I GOT YOU A PRESENT FROM THE SKATE SHOP.
RAINBOW SOCKS! JUST LIKE THE ONES RAINBOW BITE WAS WEARING!
Sock Dreams
NICOLE STAYED WITH ME WHILE I WASHED MY FACE. I DRIED MY EYES WITH MY NEW SOCKS—THEY WERE SOFT AND COOL ON MY FACE.
THAT'S THE KIND OF BEST FRIEND NICOLE IS—I MEAN, **WAS**.

HOW WAS SKATING?
FUN!
OK.
DO I HAVE ANY CHANGE LEFT?
OH, I, UH... SPENT IT AT THE SNACK BAR.
WHILE NICOLE AND HER MOM ARGUED, I SAT THINKING IN THE BACKSEAT.
NICOLE? DO YOU THINK EVERYONE'S GOING TO BE REALLY GOOD AT SKATE CAMP?
SKATE CAMP? WHAT'S THIS, NOW?

YOU DIDN'T...YOU DIDN'T TELL HER?
I, UM...
IT'S A ROLLER DERBY BOOT CAMP! YOU GET TO SKATE AND...
ROLLER DERBY?! HA! I'M SURPRISED YOUR MOTHER WOULD LET YOU DO THAT!
SERIOUSLY, ROLLER DERBY? YOU'RE NOT EXACTLY WHAT I'D CALL A BIG BRUISER TYPE.
WELL, ACTUALLY, NICOLE AND I...
MOM! I... I JUST REMEMBERED. I HAVE TO GIVE MISS KENDALL A CHECK TODAY FOR MY COSTUME.
I SAT IN SILENCE THE REST OF THE WAY TO NICOLE'S BALLET STUDIO.

UGGH, THERE'S RACHEL. I CAN'T BELIEVE WE HAVE TO GO TO JUNIOR HIGH WITH HER NEXT YEAR.
NICOLE! MRS. B.! HI!
RACHEL TRANSFERRED TO A NEW ELEMENTARY SCHOOL IN THIRD GRADE. BEST DAY OF MY LIFE.
SHE'S NOT AS BAD AS SHE USED TO BE. YOU SHOULD GIVE HER ANOTHER CHANCE.
HA!
HEY, RACHEL.
RACHEL, HONEY! SO GOOD TO SEE YOU!
OH, HI ASTRID. WHAT ARE **YOU** DOING HERE?
SNORT
NICOLE, AREN'T YOU SOOOOO EXCITED ABOUT DANCE CAMP?
UM, WELL...
DANCE CAMP?

6 WEEKS, STARTING NEXT MONTH! WE FINALLY GET TO GO ON POINTE! "POINTE" IS WHEN...
I **KNOW** WHAT POINTE IS. I'VE ONLY BEEN BEST FRIENDS WITH NICOLE MY ENTIRE LIFE.
OOOOKAY...
RACHEL, HAVE YOU SEEN OUR NEW COSTUMES YET?
MAYBE I'M PSYCHIC, BUT AS NICOLE & RACHEL GOT FARTHER & FARTHER AWAY FROM ME IN THAT PARKING LOT...
Northwest Dance Academy
I GOT A VERY BAD FEELING THAT THIS SUMMER WASN'T GOING TO GO THE WAY I PLANNED.

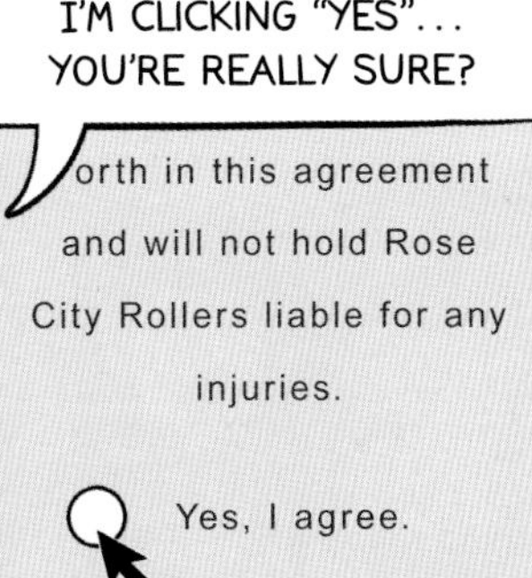

WAS I SURE? I PRETTY MUCH STUNK AT SKATING. NICOLE WAS ACTING REALLY WEIRD. BUT...

I'M SURE.

I THINK.

EVEN THOUGH NOTHING WAS **WRONG**... I STILL KIND OF AVOIDED NICOLE FOR A FEW DAYS FOR SOME REASON. **THAT** GOT BORING REAL QUICK.
YOU'RE STILL WATCHING TV? IT WAS ON WHEN I LEFT THIS MORNING!
WELL, ENJOY IT WHILE YOU CAN—I GOT YOUR LIST OF SUPPLIES FOR DERBY CAMP TODAY!
AND I GOT YOU A PRESENT. BECAUSE I AM A WONDERFUL MOTHER.
IN YOUR FAVORITE COLOR TOO!
OH...WOW. THANKS, MOM!

WE'LL RENT THE REST OF YOUR EQUIPMENT— THAT JUST LEAVES A MOUTHGUARD AND A WATER BOTTLE.
MY LITTLE ROLLER GIRL. DO YOU LIKE IT?
I DID. I LIKED IT. I WAS STARTING TO FEEL BETTER THAN I HAD ALL WEEK. UNTIL...
WHY DON'T YOU WEAR IT TO RIDE YOUR BIKE OVER TO NICOLE'S HOUSE?
OH... I DON'T WANT TO RUIN IT OR ANYTHING.
DON'T BE SILLY— IT'S A **HELMET**. YOU'VE BEEN COOPED UP ALL DAY— GO GET SOME FRESH AIR.
PARENTS ALWAYS SAY "GO GET SOME FRESH AIR," LIKE GETTING KICKED OUT OF THE HOUSE IS A REAL TREAT.
REEDWAY APTS

I DIDN'T EXACTLY MEAN TO...

BUT SOMEHOW,

I ENDED UP RIDING BY NICOLE'S HOUSE...

FOUR TIMES.

UNTIL SHE CAME OUT.
HEY.
HEY.

I LIKE YOUR HELMET.
MY MOM GOT IT FOR ME. FOR SKATE CAMP.
OH.
MAYBE WE COULD DECORATE OUR HELMETS TOGETHER!
ASTRID...
YOU COULD HELP ME PAINT A RAINBOW ON MINE— YOU'RE A BETTER ARTIST THAN I AM!
YOU COULD PAINT BALLET SLIPPERS ON YOURS!
ASTRID!

I'M NOT GOING TO DERBY CAMP.

HAVE YOU EVER PLAYED KICKBALL? YOU'RE IN THE OUTFIELD. SOME KID COMES UP TO THE PLATE AND KICKS THE BALL RIGHT AT YOU. YOU YELL, "I GOT IT! I GOT IT!" AND YOU RUN UP TO CATCH IT AND...

...IT HITS YOU RIGHT IN THE GUTS.

YEAH, THAT'S HOW I FELT NOW.

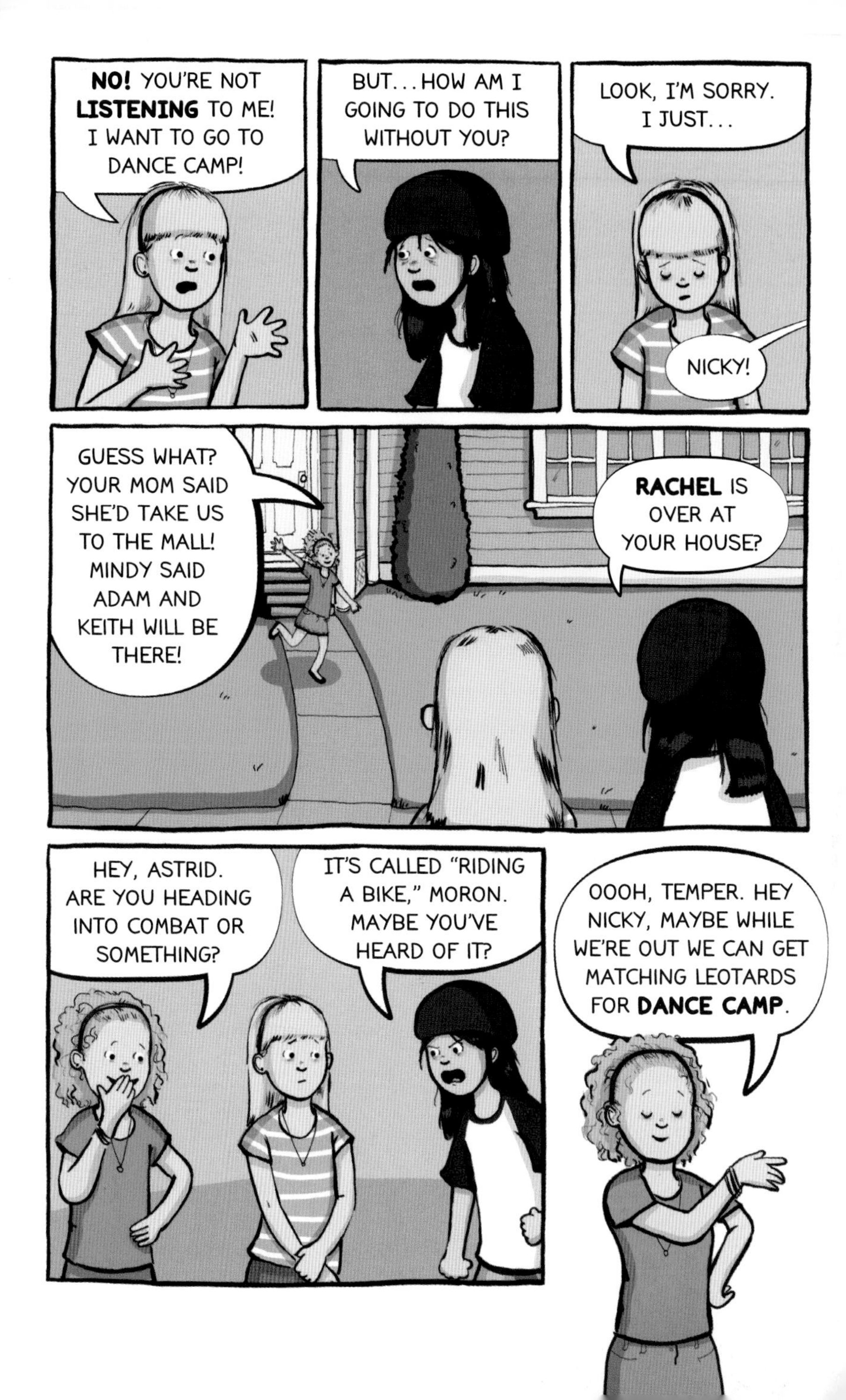
NO! YOU'RE NOT LISTENING TO ME! I WANT TO GO TO DANCE CAMP!
BUT...HOW AM I GOING TO DO THIS WITHOUT YOU?
LOOK, I'M SORRY. I JUST...
NICKY!
GUESS WHAT? YOUR MOM SAID SHE'D TAKE US TO THE MALL! MINDY SAID ADAM AND KEITH WILL BE THERE!
RACHEL IS OVER AT YOUR HOUSE?
HEY, ASTRID. ARE YOU HEADING INTO COMBAT OR SOMETHING?
IT'S CALLED "RIDING A BIKE," MORON. MAYBE YOU'VE HEARD OF IT?
OOOH, TEMPER. HEY NICKY, MAYBE WHILE WE'RE OUT WE CAN GET MATCHING LEOTARDS FOR DANCE CAMP.

DO YOU... WANT TO COME TO THE MALL WITH US?
SNORT
I CAN'T BELIEVE YOU INVITED HER TO THE MALL. WHAT WOULD SHE BUY— MORE BAGGY SHORTS?
I PEDALED OUT OF THERE FAST BEFORE I COULD HEAR WHAT NICOLE SAID BACK... IF SHE SAID ANYTHING AT ALL.
MAYBE I **WAS** GOING INTO COMBAT... AND IT LOOKED LIKE I WAS HEADING IN ALL ALONE.

CHAPTER 5
NOT-SO-FUN FACT: PREPARING FOR ROLLER DERBY BOOT CAMP IS A LOT LESS FUN WITHOUT A BEST FRIEND.
JUNE
FINALLY... IT WAS TIME.
SLAM!
THERE'S MY ROLLER GIRL! *SIGH* YOU LOOK OLDER ALREADY!

NICOLE'S MOM IS STILL GOING TO DRIVE YOU HOME, RIGHT?
GENTLE READERS, I'D LIKE TO PAUSE HERE FOR A MOMENT. IT MIGHT SURPRISE YOU THAT I HADN'T MENTIONED A CERTAIN LITTLE FACT TO MY MOTHER. BUT WHAT WOULD YOU SAY IN MY POSITION?
Pause
"ACTUALLY, MY BEST FRIEND DITCHED ME FOR A RAT-FACED JERK, AND NOW I'M HEADING INTO THIS, THE SCARIEST DAY OF MY LIFE, ALL ALONE."
OR WOULD YOU SAY...
NOD
YES, EVERYTHING'S FINE! GOOD DEAL! GOOD DEAL!
WHAT DID I NEED NICOLE FOR, ANYWAY? A RIDE? I KNEW MY WAY HOME...
GULP
...I THINK.

I PACKED YOU A BANANA AND SOME RAISINS FOR A SNACK.
I GOT THIS.
I ALSO PUT $10 IN YOUR BAG FOR EMERGENCIES— THAT SHOULD LAST YOU THE WEEK.
I GOT THIS.
CALL ME AT WORK IF YOU NEED TO.
I GOT THIS.

OH, CRUD.
Rollers
Home of the
Rose City Rollers

HEY! DO YOU PLAN ON STANDING OUT HERE ALL DAY?
I'M HEIDI GO SEEK. I'M ONE OF YOUR COACHES.
EXIT
I'M ASTRID.
ASTRID VASQUEZ? YUP, I'VE GOT YOU HERE ON MY LIST. YOU'RE RENTING EQUIPMENT, RIGHT? JUST HEAD OVER TO THAT BOX AND GRAB SOME GEAR.
UM, EXCUSE ME, HEIDI?
THIS IS THE **JUNIOR** DERBY CAMP, RIGHT?
HA! DON'T WORRY— THEY JUST **THINK** THEY'RE ADULTS.
EVERYONE ELSE LOOKED LIKE FULL-ON GROWN-UPS.
PIERCINGS,
DYED HAIR,
MAKEUP,
. . . OTHER ASSETS.
WHERE WERE THE OTHER **KIDS**?

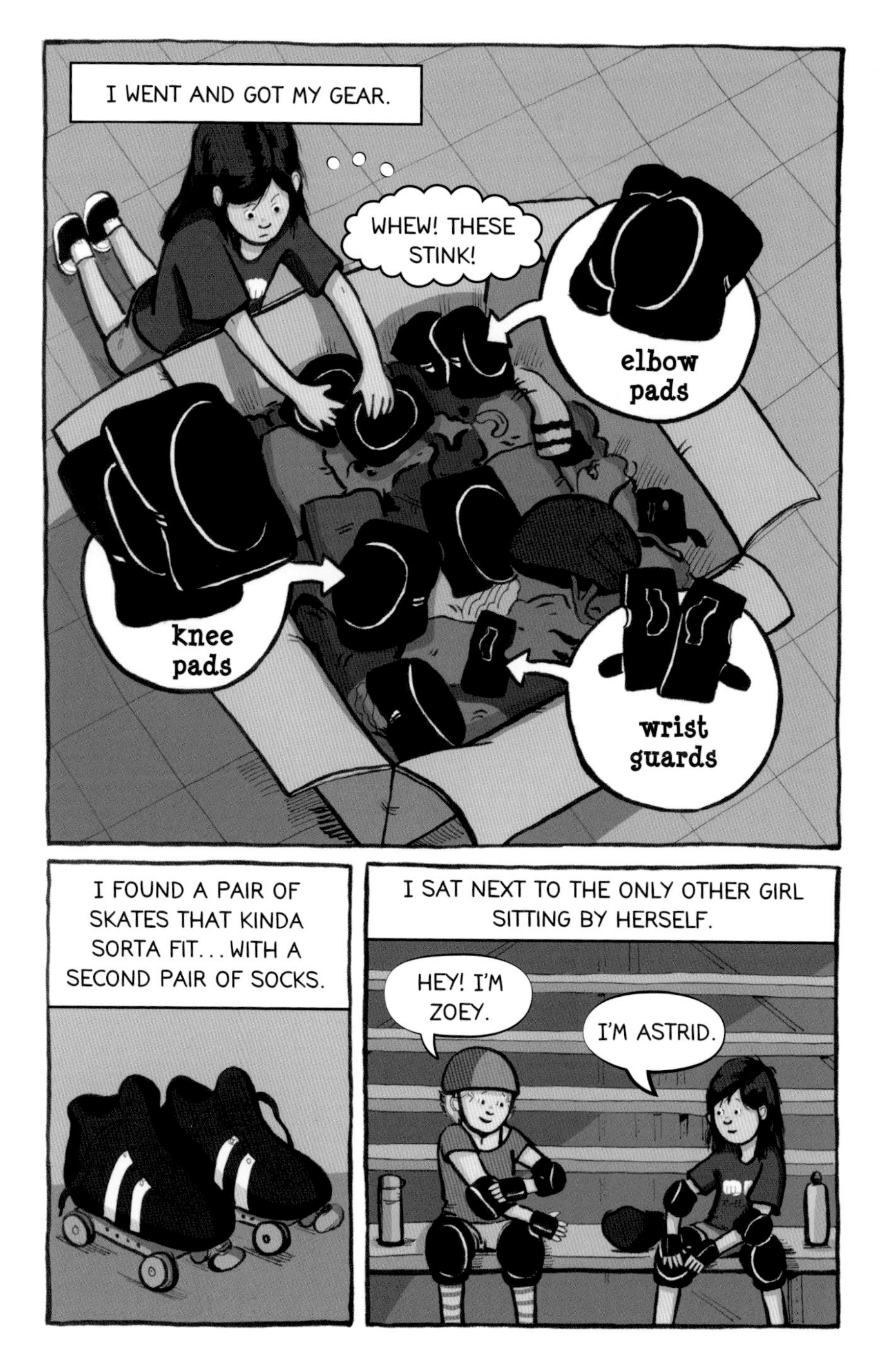
I WENT AND GOT MY GEAR.
WHEW! THESE STINK!
elbow pads
knee pads
wrist guards
I FOUND A PAIR OF SKATES THAT KINDA SORTA FIT. . . WITH A SECOND PAIR OF SOCKS.
I SAT NEXT TO THE ONLY OTHER GIRL SITTING BY HERSELF.
HEY! I'M ZOEY.
I'M ASTRID.

YOU'RE NEW TO DERBY, HUH.
MAYBE... WHY?
YOUR WRIST GUARDS ARE ON BACKWARD.
OH.
TWEET!
EVERYONE TO THE CENTER OF THE TRACK!
OK, FIRST DRILL...
SHUFFLE
PSST! NO "GET TO KNOW YOU" SESSION FIRST?
WELCOME TO THE BIG LEAGUES.
THE 50-LAP KILLER!
THE 50-LAP **WHAT?!**

I WANT A SINGLE-FILE LINE BEHIND ME ON THE TRACK.
FASTER SKATERS UP FRONT.
SO, NEW GIRL'S FAST, HUH!
!
EVERYONE READY? HERE WE GO, ON THE WHISTLE!
TWEET!
THUNK
HOLD UP, HOLD UP. IF YOU'RE **NEW**, PLEASE DO YOUR LAPS ON THE OUTSIDE OF THE TRACK FOR NOW.

GASP
PANT
GASP
PANT
PANT
GASP
PANT
GASP
AFTER WHAT SEEMED LIKE FOREVER...
ONE... *PANT*... LAP... *PANT*
50 LAPS! NICE WORK, LADIES!
BRING IT IN AND GET SOME WATER!

MOST OF YOU KNOW ME— I'M HEIDI GO SEEK.
THIS IS NAPOLEON BLOWNAPART— SHE'LL BE YOUR OTHER COACH.
LET'S GO AROUND AND INTRODUCE YOURSELVES, SHALL WE?
I'M BRAIDY PUNCH. WATCH THE BRAIDS.
I'M SLAMWICH.
SCREAM SODA.
BALD TO THE BONE.
REDICULOUS.
I'M PANDA-MONIUM.
I'M MARZ ROLLVER.
THRILLA GODZILLA.
DRACULOLA.
I'M RUTHLESS.
BACON LIL' HEARTS.
BLONDILOCKS!
I'M MINNIE ME!
LITTLE BONEBREAKER.
WELL, I'M THINKING "SLAY MISERABLES," OR MAYBE "PHANTOM"... I HAVEN'T DECIDED. SO, JUST ZOEY FOR NOW.
I'M... JUST ASTRID.

YOU MIGHT WANT TO WORK ON THAT SKATE NAME, "JUST ASTRID." OK, I KNOW A LOT OF YOU HAVE BEEN SKATING WITH ROSEBUDS FOR A WHILE, BUT WE'RE STILL GOING TO START OFF WITH SOME BASICS.
GROAN
GROAN
GROAN
WHEN DO WE START **HITTING**?
GULP.
FIRST UP. . . FALLING!
HEY! I CAN **DO** FALLING!
THIS IS IMPORTANT BECAUSE WHEN WE GET TO HITTING— **BRAIDY**— YOU NEED TO KNOW HOW TO FALL SAFELY TO AVOID GETTING HURT.

ONE WHISTLE... ONE-KNEE FALL.
TWO WHISTLES... TWO-KNEE FALL.
THREE WHISTLES... FALL SMALL.
THIS IS THE **MOST IMPORTANT**. WHEN YOU FALL DURING A BOUT, TUCK YOURSELF INTO A LITTLE BALL SO YOU DON'T GET RUN OVER.
EVERYONE READY? ON THE TRACK!
TWEET!
TWEET TWEET!
TWEET!
TWEET TWEET!
TWEET!
TWEET TWEET TWEET!
TWEET TWEET TWEET!
TWEET!
TWEET!
TWEET TWEET!
TWEET!
TWEET TWEET TWEET!
TWEET!
TWEET!

OK, I THINK THAT'S PRETTY GOOD FOR A WARM-UP.
WARM-UP?!?
NEXT DRILL! EVERYONE LINE UP BEHIND NAPOLEON.
I'VE NEVER BEEN SO TIRED BEFORE IN MY ENTIRE LIFE! HOW AM I GOING TO SURVIVE TWO MORE HOURS OF THIS?!
EXCEPT YOU, ASTRID. COME WITH ME.

WHAT I WANT **YOU** TO WORK ON ARE YOUR **CROSSOVERS**.
CROSSOVERS ARE WHAT GET YOU GOING REALLY FAST THROUGH THE CORNERS.
START WITH YOUR FEET PARALLEL...
THEN... CROSS OVER!
THUNK
NO PROBLEM! JUST TRY AGAIN!
STAND... AND...
...CROSS OVER!
THUNK

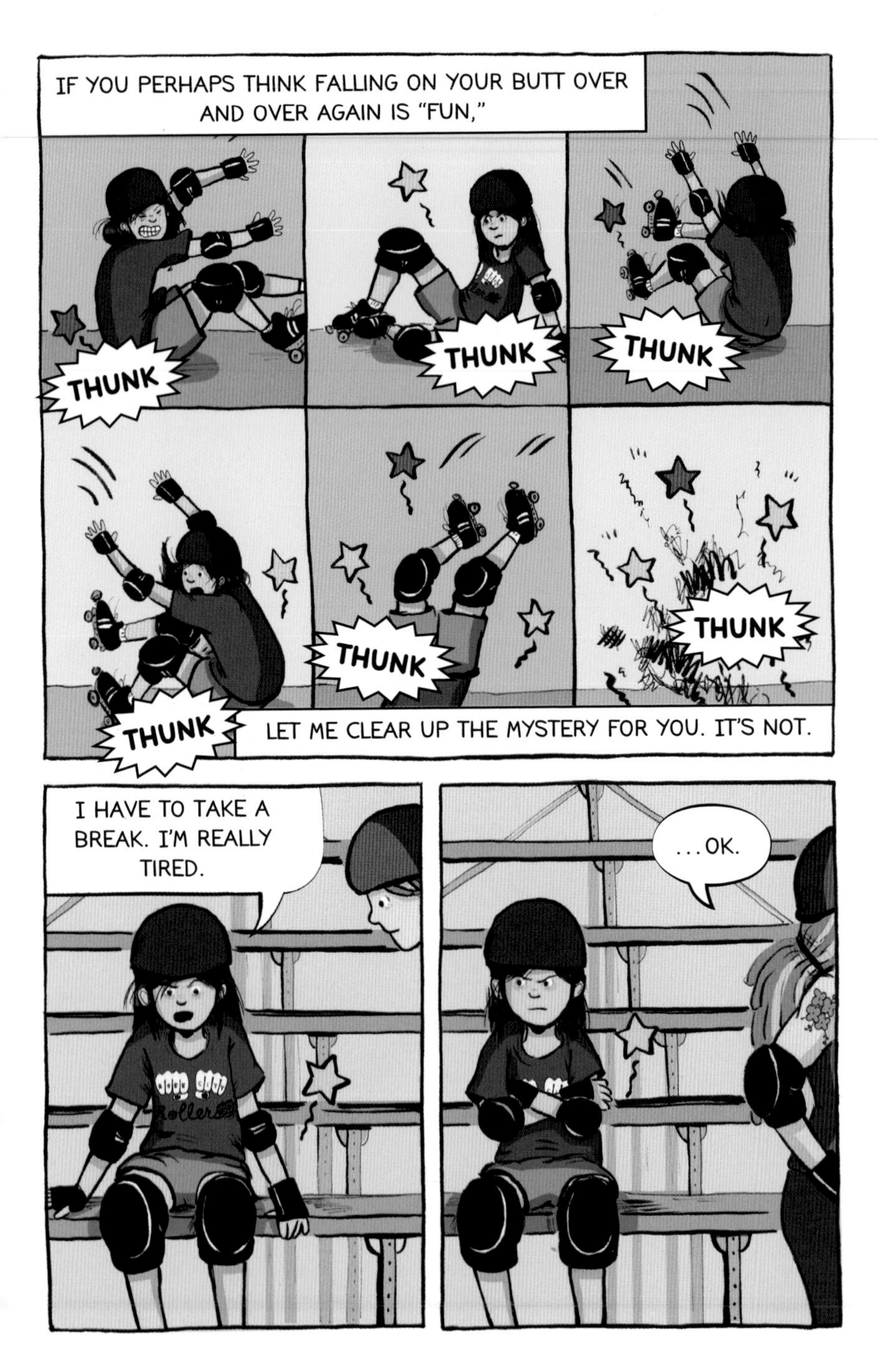
IF YOU PERHAPS THINK FALLING ON YOUR BUTT OVER AND OVER AGAIN IS "FUN,"
THUNK
THUNK
THUNK
THUNK
THUNK
THUNK
LET ME CLEAR UP THE MYSTERY FOR YOU. IT'S NOT.
I HAVE TO TAKE A BREAK. I'M REALLY TIRED.
...OK.

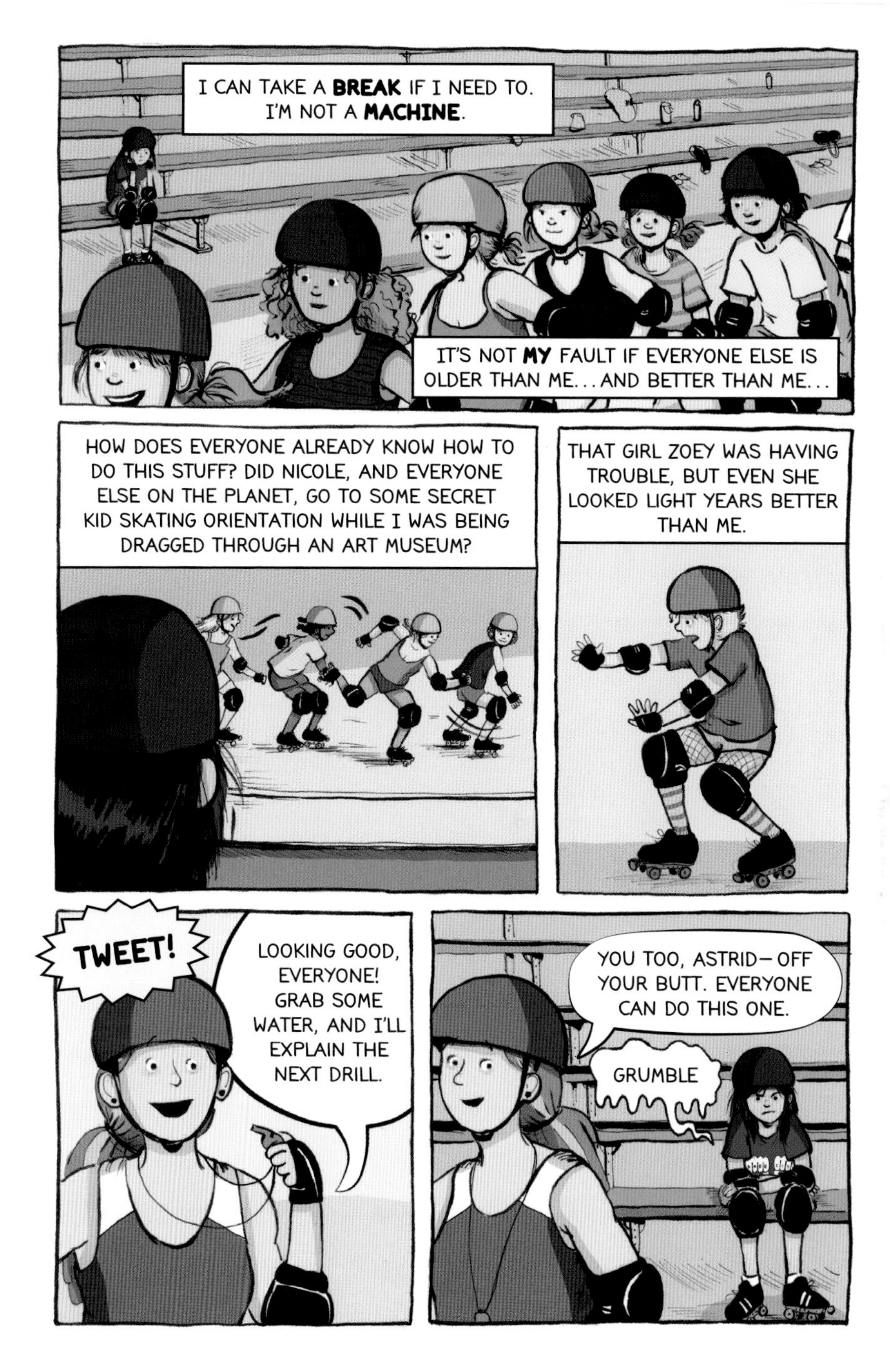
I CAN TAKE A **BREAK** IF I NEED TO. I'M NOT A **MACHINE**.
IT'S NOT **MY** FAULT IF EVERYONE ELSE IS OLDER THAN ME... AND BETTER THAN ME...
HOW DOES EVERYONE ALREADY KNOW HOW TO DO THIS STUFF? DID NICOLE, AND EVERYONE ELSE ON THE PLANET, GO TO SOME SECRET KID SKATING ORIENTATION WHILE I WAS BEING DRAGGED THROUGH AN ART MUSEUM?
THAT GIRL ZOEY WAS HAVING TROUBLE, BUT EVEN SHE LOOKED LIGHT YEARS BETTER THAN ME.
TWEET!
LOOKING GOOD, EVERYONE! GRAB SOME WATER, AND I'LL EXPLAIN THE NEXT DRILL.
YOU TOO, ASTRID— OFF YOUR BUTT. EVERYONE CAN DO THIS ONE.
GRUMBLE

OKAY, THIS IS AN ENDURANCE DRILL. WE'RE WORKING ON YOUR STRENGTH AND STAMINA. THIS ONE IS SUPPOSED TO BE HARD!
THERE'S A SURPRISE.
THIS IS A **PUSHCART** DRILL. FIND A PARTNER AND PUT YOUR HANDS ON HER LOWER BACK. YOU'RE GOING TO PUSH HER AROUND THE TRACK, LIKE THIS. GOT IT? ONE MINUTE, THEN YOU SWITCH.
EVERYONE HAVE A PARTNER?
SORRY YOU GOT STUCK WITH ME. I'M NOT GOING TO BE VERY GOOD AT THIS.
NO ONE IS GOOD AT THIS— IT'S TORTURE.

ONE MINUTE STARTS... NOW!
TWEET!
YOU HAVE TO SORT OF—**PUSH** TO THE SIDE.
I'M (PUFF)
TRYING! (HUFF)
THERE YOU GO! WE'RE MOVING!
THIS IS SO EMBARRASSING. I CAN'T EVEN SKATE WHEN I'M HOLDING ON TO SOMEONE ELSE.
DID SHE FORGET TO TIME THIS? IT MUST BE AT LEAST 3 MINUTES BY NOW. OR 4. OR...
THIRTY SECONDS!
ONLY THIRTY SECONDS?! I FELT LIKE I HAD BEEN SKATING FOR ALL ETERNITY.
SO. TIRED. CAN'T. MOVE. LEGS. ANYMORE...

FINALLY, **FINALLY**...
ONE MINUTE! SWITCH PLACES!
ANNND, GO!
TWEET!
I DIDN'T THINK ZOEY WAS THAT FAST, BUT SHE TOOK OFF LIKE A SHOT!
WHOA! HEY! SLOW DOWN, SLOW DOWN!
OK! I'M SORRY! I'M TRYING!
I CAN'T TURN! I CAN'T TURN!
AAAAAGHHHHHHH

ASTRID, ARE YOU ALL RIGHT?
TWEET!
I'M SORRY, I DIDN'T THINK I WAS GOING THAT FAST!

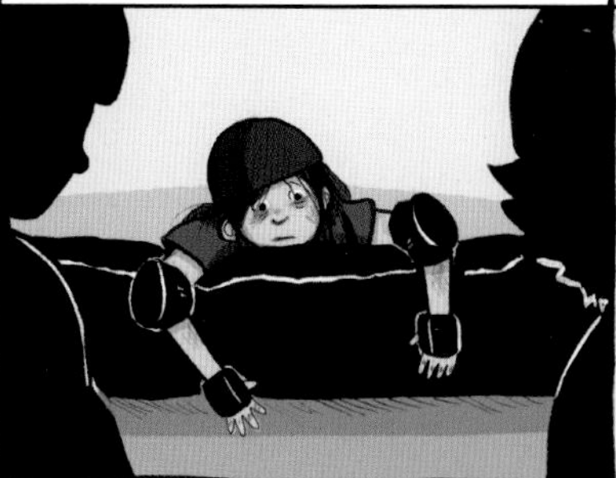
EVERYONE WAS SILENT AND STARING AT ME. MY LEGS WERE SHAKING, MY KNUCKLES WERE BLEEDING, AND ALL IN ALL I WAS A TOTAL AND USELESS FAILURE AT ROLLER DERBY. THERE WAS ONLY ONE THING TO SAY...

WAAAAAHH!

HEIDI TOOK MY SKATES AND HELMET OFF, AND ZOEY GOT ME AN ICE PACK. I SAT ON THE BLEACHERS FOR THE REST OF PRACTICE, FEELING LIKE A COMPLETE IDIOT.
IF NICOLE WERE HERE, SHE'D BE SITTING NEXT TO ME, MAKING ME FEEL BETTER & TRYING TO GET ME TO LAUGH.

FINALLY— PRACTICE WAS OVER.
NICE WORK, LADIES! SAME TIME, SAME PLACE TOMORROW!
ASTRID, WAIT UP.
I KNOW THIS WAS A TOUGH FIRST DAY FOR YOU. REMEMBER, A LOT OF THESE GIRLS HAVE BEEN SKATING FOR 5, 6 MONTHS WITH THE ROSEBUDS ALREADY. IT WILL GET BETTER, I PROMISE.
ASTRID, ARE YOU FEELING BETTER? I'M SORRY, AGAIN...
EXIT
I BRUSHED PAST ZOEY, MUMBLING SOMETHING LIKE "SDKJFMOLSDM." RUDE, I KNOW, BUT WHEN THOSE TEARS GET GOING, THEY JUST WON'T STOP.
I JUST WANTED TO GET HOME, FALL INTO MY BED, AND NEVER GET UP AGAIN.

30 MINUTES LATER, I CHANGED MY WISH—I JUST WANTED TO **GET HOME**.
SE BIDWELL
SE 11 AVE
I'M **PRETTY** SURE THIS IS THE STREET...
THAT HOUSE LOOKS FAMILIAR...
IT'S FUNNY HOW A NORMAL SUNNY DAY CAN TURN INTO "SCORCHING HOT SAHARA DESERT" **REALLY** FAST.
THROW IN MY ACHING MUSCLES & SOME NEW BLISTERS ON MY FEET, AND SOON I FELT LIKE LAWRENCE OF ARABIA*
*EVENING OF CULTURAL ENLIGHTENMENT, CIRCA 4TH GRADE. NOT RECOMMENDED.
COMPLETE WITH MIRAGES...
WATER? WATER?

CIVILIZATION!
E-Z STOP
E-Z STOP
AAAAAAAHHHHHHHHHHH
THE REFRESHING BREEZE OF COOL AIR-CONDITIONING. THE SWEET, SWEET SMELL OF CANDY AND GUM.
I USED MY EMERGENCY FUNDS, BECAUSE THIS QUALIFIED AS A DEFINITE EMERGENCY.
Sugar Busters
WOW... YOU MUST HAVE BEEN REALLY THIRSTY.
YOU HAVE NO IDEA.
OREGON LOTTERY

AT LEAST NOW I KNEW WHERE I WAS.
I FORGOT ABOUT THIS HIGHWAY...
I JUST HAD TO CLIMB HEART ATTACK HILL...
...AND I WAS HOME.
KISS
I REMEMBER STUMBLING INTO THE LIVING ROOM AND THEN...
...NOTHING.

ASTRID?
ASTRID, HONEY? WAKE UP, IT'S DINNER TIME!
I BROUGHT HOME PAD THAI TO CELEBRATE YOUR FIRST DAY AT CAMP!
SO, TELL ME EVERYTHING! HOW WAS IT? DID YOU MAKE ANY NEW FRIENDS? DID YOU HAVE A GOOD TIME?
SHUFFLE
...WHY ARE YOU WALKING SO FUNNY?
UGGH, ASTRID, TABLE MANNERS!
SLORP
SO?
JUST A QUESTION, FOR NO PARTICULAR REASON... WHAT'S THE RETURN POLICY ON THE MONEY YOU PAID FOR CAMP?

OH, HONEY... WAS IT THAT BAD? DID YOU HATE IT THAT MUCH?
I DIDN'T **HATE** IT, IT'S JUST...
HOW DID NICOLE LIKE IT? MAYBE I SHOULD TALK TO HER MOM, SEE WHAT SHE THINKS ABOUT IT...
NO! I WAS JUST... **WONDERING!** FOR CURIOSITY'S SAKE. NICOLE AND I HAD A GRAND TIME. JUST GRAND.
NOW IF YOU'LL EXCUSE ME, I'M FULL, SO I BELIEVE I'LL LIE DOWN FOR A SPELL. IF THAT'S OK WITH YOU, MOTHER DEAREST.
?
THE LAST THING I REMEMBER BEFORE DRIFTING OFF WAS RAINBOW BITE'S SMARMY FACE STARING DOWN AT ME.
ROLLER DERBY
THANKS A LOT, RAINBOW BITE. THANKS... A... ZZZZZZZZZZZZZZZZZZZZ

CHAPTER 6
IF ANYTHING, I FELT EVEN MORE NERVOUS FOR MY SECOND DAY OF DERBY CAMP. NOW EVERYONE **KNEW** I WAS A LOSER.
YOU'RE BACK! I KNEW IT! SOME OF THE OTHER GIRLS SAID NO— BUT I KNEW IT. HOW ARE YOU FEELING?
I'M... OK.
LISTEN, EVERYONE HAS A HARD TIME ON THEIR FIRST DAY. IT'S LIKE A RITE OF PASSAGE.
YEAH, BUT DOES EVERYONE **CRY** ON THEIR FIRST DAY?
I CRIED FOR MY FIRST **WEEK**.
ME TOO!
ME TOO!
I BARFED ON MY FIRST DAY OF PRACTICE DURING THE 50-LAP KILLER. RIGHT ON THE TRACK TOO— I COULDN'T MAKE IT OUTSIDE IN TIME.
I REMEMBER! THAT WAS **HILARIOUS**!

AND HERE, I BROUGHT YOU A PRESENT. TO SAY SORRY FOR KNOCKING YOU INTO THE BLEACHERS. ALSO, SO YOU WON'T BE MAD AND SUE THE PANTS OFF OF ME.
NO...
I WOULDN'T DO THAT.
GOOD!
UM, ZOEY? WHAT... IS IT?
IT'S A STICKER OF HUGH JACKMAN, WITH HAND-CRAFTED GLITTER HAIR, OBVIOUSLY!
TWEET!
(SIGH) AND SO IT BEGINS AGAIN...

I WISH I COULD SAY I TRIED REALLY HARD AND GOT BETTER AT SKATING... BUT I STILL PRETTY MUCH STUNK. EVERY DRILL WAS A FALLING DRILL FOR ME.
CROSSOVERS...
THUNK
PLOW STOPS...
THUNK
...BACKWARD SKATING.
THUNK
REMEMBER, IF YOU'RE GOING TO FALL... FALL SMALL!
EACH AFTERNOON, I CAPPED OFF MY WONDERFUL DAY WITH AN HOUR-LONG HIKE THROUGH THE BLAZING SUN.
BY 7 PM, I WAS INSTANTLY ASLEEP— EXCEPT FOR WAKING MYSELF UP WITH THE BRUISES.
OW.

ON THURSDAY, AFTER ANOTHER WILDLY SUCCESSFUL DAY OF FALLING,
OW.
I WAS PUTTING MY GEAR AWAY WHEN I SAW IT.
I MOVED THE GEAR BOX BACK BY THE LOCKERS!
!
WHOA.
WAS THIS ACTUALLY HER LOCKER??
Rainbow Bite
ASTRID!
I WASN'T! I DIDN'T...!
RELAX, GIRLFRIEND. I WAS JUST GOING TO SAY THAT I SAW YOU WALKING HOME YESTERDAY.
OH, WELL, I LIVE REALLY CLOSE BY, IT'S NO BIG DEAL.

YOU KNOW, YOU CAN ALWAYS BRING THOSE SKATES HOME WITH YOU TO PRACTICE AT NIGHT. YOU COULD EVEN SKATE HOME—OUTDOOR SKATING IS REALLY GOOD PRACTICE FOR DERBY.
THAT DOESN'T SOUND LIKE THE SAFEST IDEA TO ME. YOU'VE SEEN ME SKATE IN HERE—I'D PROBABLY MAKE IT HALF A BLOCK BEFORE I GOT HIT BY AN 18-WHEELER.
HMMM. LET ME THINK ON THIS. I'LL GET BACK TO YOU.
SHE HAD A FARAWAY LOOK IN HER EYES, LIKE WHEN MOM IS HATCHING A NEW EVIL PLAN TO RUIN MY LIFE. I SMELLED TROUBLE.
OK, YOU KEEP THINKING, HEIDI! I'LL SEE YOU LATER!
I RAN OUT OF THERE AS FAST AS MY BROKEN, DEAD LEGS COULD CARRY ME.

CHAPTER 7
I DIDN'T HAVE LONG TO WAIT UNTIL HEIDI UNLEASHED HER EVIL PLAN.
WE'RE DOING SOMETHING DIFFERENT TODAY! COME AND GET SOME SUNSCREEN . . .
WE'RE GOING OUTDOOR SKATING!
IT'S LIKE A HUNDRED DEGREES OUT THERE!
I'LL GET SUNSTROKE!
OH, COME ON. NO ONE'S GOING TO DIE.
I'M NOT SO SURE ABOUT THAT.
THERE'S A BIKE PATH THAT RUNS ALONG THE RIVER. WE CUT THROUGH THE AMUSEMENT PARK TO GET THERE.

DO YOU PLAY ROLLER DERBY?
UM, YEAH.
WOW. MOM, DID YOU HEAR THAT? SHE PLAYS **ROLLER DERBY**!
I'M LUCKY I'VE BEEN HIKING THROUGH THE SAHARA EVERY DAY— AT LEAST I'M PREPARED FOR THE HEAT. WHAT WITH THE COMPLAINING & STOPPING FOR WATER, I'M ALMOST ABLE TO KEEP UP.
AT THIS POINT IN THE STORY, I SHOULD PROBABLY MENTION ONE LITTLE FACT ABOUT MY SKATING...
OK EVERYONE, WE'RE AT OUR FIRST HILL. THE KEY TO GOING DOWN HILLS IS TO USE YOUR PLOW STOP. WE'RE GOING TO START SLOWLY— I'LL GO FIRST TO DEMONST—
THAT LITTLE FACT BEING...

I'M NOT SO GREAT AT STOPPING.
AAAAAAAAAAAGGHHHHHH!!!!
GET LOW!
PLOW STOP! PLOW STOP!
CRASH!
ASTRID!
ARE YOU OK?
I FELL SMALL!
OH MY GOSH, THAT WAS INSANE!
THAT WAS **AMAZING**!
THANKS, ASTRID, FOR MY DAILY HEART ATTACK.

I CAN'T REALLY EXPLAIN IT... BUT I FELT GREAT AFTER THAT! I HAD LOOKED DANGER STRAIGHT IN THE EYE– AND I SURVIVED!
WOW. I DIDN'T KNOW I COULD SKATE PRACTICALLY DOWNTOWN!
ME NEITHER! THIS IS AWESOME– I'M STILL 3 YEARS AWAY FROM MY DRIVER'S LICENCE! NOW... I DON'T NEED ONE!

WE STOPPED FOR POPSICLES IN A PARK ALONGSIDE THE RIVER.
DUDE, WHO KNEW ASTRID WAS SUCH A SPEED DEMON?
SHE WAS LIKE EVEL KNIEVEL GOING DOWN THAT HILL!
OR LIKE RAINBOW BITE!
I JUST LICKED MY POPSICLE, FEELING HAPPIER THAN I HAD IN WEEKS.
MY GOOD MOOD LASTED THE ENTIRE PRACTICE.
I THINK I **WILL** TAKE MY SKATES HOME FOR THE WEEKEND!
GOOD FOR YOU!
Rainbow Bite
MAYBE I WAS HAPPY AFTER FINALLY HAVING A GOOD DAY OF PRACTICE. MAYBE I HAD SUNSTROKE. WHATEVER IT WAS, I WAS SUDDENLY STRUCK WITH A CRAZY IDEA.
Rainbow Bite

Dear Rainbow Bite,
I think you're the best
skater who has ever
rolled around the
planet. You're awesome.
I hope to skate like you
some day.
Sincerely,
A Rose Dud
Rainbow Bite
SHOVE
Sharpie
PERMANENT

I WAS PRETTY PROUD OF MYSELF FOR THINKING OF THAT ROSEBUD-ROSE DUD JOKE JUST LIKE THAT!
YOU SKATE HOME? COOOOOL! I WANT TO TRY THAT! HAVE A GOOD WEEKEND, EVEL KNIEVEL!
YOU TOO!
E-Z STOP
SKATING HOME CUT MY COMMUTE TIME DOWN TO 30 MINUTES! I DIDN'T EVEN NEED TO STOP FOR EMERGENCY RATIONS.
THAT, AND I'D ALREADY SPENT MY WEEKLY $10.
IT WAS FUN HAVING MY SKATES FOR THE WEEKEND! I PRACTICED MY...
T-STOPS,
PLOW STOPS,
EVEN MY TURN-AROUND TOE STOPS (THANKS TO THE COUCH).

MOM WAS SO IMPRESSED WITH MY HELPFULNESS AROUND OUR APARTMENT, I CAME UP WITH A NEW AD CAMPAIGN.
HEY KIDS! DO YOU FIND DOING CHORES A TOTAL DRAG? INTRODUCING...
ROLLER SKATES!
A NEW, FUN WAY TO DO YOUR WORK AROUND THE HOUSE!
DO YOUR CHORES IN A FLASH!
MAKE CLEANING A BREEZE!
NO.
ORDER NOW!

CHAPTER 8
BELIEVE IT OR NOT, WHEN MONDAY MORNING CAME AROUND, I WAS ACTUALLY LOOKING FORWARD TO DERBY CAMP!
GOOD MORNING TO YOU, MOTHER, ON THIS LOVELY AND BEAUTIFUL DAY! READY TO GO?
GOOD MORNING TO YOU TOO, SUNSHINE!
UUUGGHGH! WHAT IS THAT SMELL?!
IT'S YOUR SHIRT! DID YOU STORE IT IN A DUMPSTER ALL WEEKEND?
NO! IT WAS IN MY ROOM!
SWEATY GEAR
OLD SOCKS
SHIRT
IT DOESN'T STINK THAT BAD!
YES, IT DOES. LISTEN, KIDS CAN BE CRUEL IN JUNIOR HIGH, ESPECIALLY IF YOU SMELL BAD. WHICH REMINDS ME, I SHOULD START PICKING UP DEODORANT FOR YOU TOO.
MOOOOMMMM!

YOU'LL THANK ME, TRUST ME. NOW GO PUT ON A CLEAN SHIRT.
I DON'T **HAVE** ANY CLEAN SHIRTS!
THAT'S NOT MY FAULT. IF IT'S NOT IN THE HAMPER, IT DOESN'T GET WASHED. BESIDES, YOU HAVE THAT WHOLE BAG OF CLOTHES MRS. KEMP GAVE YOU LAST WEEK— I HAVEN'T SEEN YOU WEARING ANY OF **THOSE**.
YEAH, BECAUSE I'M NOT A COLOR-BLIND 3-YEAR-OLD.
I'LL BE IN THE CAR. YOU'VE GOT FIVE MINUTES.
GRUMBLE
MRS. KEMP WAS MY MOM'S CO-WORKER. SHE THOUGHT SHE WAS BEING NICE BY SENDING OVER HER DAUGHTER BRITTNEY'S HAND-ME-DOWNS.
BY ALL ACCOUNTS, BRITTNEY WAS 13 YEARS OLD. I DO NOT BELIEVE THIS.
SERIOUSLY, WHAT 13-YEAR-OLD WEARS THIS STUFF?
Princess
Purr-fect!
I REFUSE TO WEAR ANYTHING PINK, SO THAT RULED OUT 98% OF HER COLLECTION.

I SETTLED ON A TASTEFUL* ST. PATTY'S DAY ENSEMBLE.
HONK HONK!
*JUST KIDDING
THAT'S CUTE! IT'S NICE TO SEE YOU WEARING SOME COLOR FOR ONCE!
GRUMBLE
I WANT TO START SCHOOL SHOPPING EARLY THIS YEAR, SINCE I KNOW WHAT SHOPPING WITH YOU IS LIKE. JUNIOR HIGH IS A BIG DEAL, AND I PUT ASIDE A LITTLE EXTRA MONEY SO WE CAN GET YOU SOME CUTE CLOTHES BEFORE SCHOOL STARTS.
JOY OF JOYS.
ON MY LIST OF FUN THINGS IN LIFE, CLOTHES SHOPPING WAS PRETTY CLOSE TO DEAD LAST.
*Cavities filled by dentist.
*Stuck in a broken elevator with Rachel.
*Clothes shopping
*Death by shark attack
WHY PEOPLE ENJOYED TRYING ON A MILLION DIFFERENT OUTFITS IN A BOILING HOT DRESSING ROOM WAS BEYOND ME.

I LOVE YOU. HERE'S $10— THIS SHOULD LAST YOU THE WEEK.
GRUMBLE— THANKS.
AND ONE MORE THING...
UNZIP!
HEY!
YOU CAN'T FOOL YOUR OLD MOM. I KNOW YOU TOO WELL. NOW GET OUT OF HERE.
ROSE CITY Rollers
SCORE:
MOM: 1
ME: 0

REMEMBER WHAT I SAID ABOUT LOOKING FORWARD TO CAMP TODAY?
ERIN GO BRAGH!
YOU STOLE ME LUCKY CHARMS!
I DON'T KNOW WHAT IT WAS— MAYBE IT WAS THE LUCK OF THE IRISH— THAT MADE ME LOOK OVER AT RAINBOW BITE'S LOCKER.
WAS THAT...?
TO ROSE DUD
Hang in there, and repeat after me. Tougher. Stronger. Fearless! Signed, Rainbow Bite
MAYBE MY LUCK WAS TURNING AROUND!
TWEET TWEET!
OK LADIES, LISTEN UP! I GOT SOME EXCITING NEWS OVER THE WEEKEND. AS SOME OF YOU KNOW, THE ROSE CITY ROLLERS HAVE A GAME AGAINST SEATTLE NEXT MONTH.
WELL, THE TEAMS WOULD LIKE THE ROSEBUDS TO PUT ON A MINI-BOUT AT HALF TIME. DRUM UP INTEREST IN JUNIOR DERBY, RECRUIT SOME NEW SKATERS. WHAT DO YOU SAY?
AWESOME!
WHOA, REALLY?

THIS WILL BE DIFFERENT FROM OTHER BOUTS YOU'VE PLAYED IN. IT'S ONLY GOING TO BE HALF AN HOUR LONG, AND THERE WILL ONLY BE 8 SKATERS PER TEAM.

IN A WEEK OR TWO, WE'LL SPLIT YOU UP INTO TWO TEAMS. WE WANT YOU ALL TO PLAY, BUT FOR SOME OF YOU NEWER SKATERS...

WE'LL HAVE TO ASSESS YOUR SKILLS TO MAKE SURE YOU CAN BE SAFE ON THE TRACK.

OH MY GOSH! A REAL BOUT!!

WITH THAT IN MIND, TODAY WE'RE GOING TO START WORKING ON SOME GAME PLAY STRATEGY. AND THAT MEANS...

HITTING!

OK, ON THE TRACK—
START WARMING UP.
ASTRID...
NAPOLEON AND I HAVE BEEN TALKING. TO BE HONEST, WE'RE NOT SURE IF YOU'LL BE READY TO SKATE IN THE BOUT. WE'LL SEE HOW YOU PROGRESS IN THE NEXT FEW WEEKS, AND WE'LL MAKE A DECISION THEN.
UH-HUH!
WE CAN'T RISK YOU, OR ANYONE ELSE, GETTING HURT, SO YOU MAY NOT BE READY THIS TIME.
UH-HUH!
IF YOU'RE NOT READY FOR THIS BOUT, DON'T WORRY. KEEP SKATING WITH ROSEBUDS, AND YOU'LL GET PLENTY OF CHANCES TO BOUT. OK? DO YOU UNDERSTAND WHAT I'M SAYING?
UH-HUH!
I'M GOING TO PLAY IN MY FIRST BOUT!

OK, ONCE YOU'RE WARMED UP, PAIR UP WITH WHOEVER IS CLOSEST TO YOU ON THE TRACK.
WE'RE GOING TO DO SOME HITTING DRILLS.
WE'RE GOING TO START OFF STANDING STILL. GET DOWN LOW IN DERBY STANCE. STAND CLOSE TO YOUR PARTNER AND...
...**THROW** YOUR HIP TO THE SIDE! THIS IS YOUR BASIC HIP CHECK.
NO ELBOWS, TRIPPING, OR HITTING TO THE HEAD. THESE ARE ILLEGAL HITS AND THEY'LL SEND YOU TO THE PENALTY BOX.
IT'S YOU AND ME, PIPSQUEAK.
TOUGHER. STRONGER.
FEARLESS.
YOU CAN PRETTY MUCH JUST REPLAY THIS SCENE OVER AND OVER IN YOUR HEAD FOR 2 HOURS TO GET A SENSE OF HOW MY MORNING WENT.

TWEET TWEET!
NICE WORK, LADIES! YOU'RE LOOKING GREAT. SINCE YOU DID SUCH A GOOD JOB TODAY, WE'LL END WITH A GAME...
...LAST WOMAN STANDING.
YES!
?
YAY!
IF YOU HAVEN'T PLAYED BEFORE, IT'S PRETTY SIMPLE. EVERYONE SKATES TOGETHER ON THE TRACK. IF YOU FALL DOWN OR GET HIT OUT, YOU'RE OUT. THE LAST WOMAN STANDING IS THE WINNER.
ALL HITS MUST BE LEGAL, OR YOU'LL GO TO THE PENALTY BOX.
ALL RIGHT, SO I DIDN'T HAVE THE GREATEST MORNING WITH THE HITTING. BUT I COULD MAKE UP FOR ALL OF THAT RIGHT NOW. IF I WAS THE LAST WOMAN STANDING, THE COACHES WOULD **HAVE** TO SEE THAT I COULD...
SLAM!
YOU'RE OUT, ASTRID!

...OR I COULD BE THE FIRST WOMAN SITTING.
HOW DID THOSE GIRLS DO IT? THEY WERE SO TOUGH-LOOKING. SO FIERCE. AND HERE I WAS, FIRST WOMAN SITTING, LOOKING LIKE A DEMENTED LEPRECHAUN.
I NEED TO BE TOUGHER! I NEED TO BE STRONGER! I NEED...
...AND THEN THE ANSWER HIT ME LIKE AN 18-WHEELER. IT WAS SO OBVIOUS!
I NEED TO DYE MY HAIR!

I MADE MY MOVE AFTER PRACTICE.
ZOEY? CAN I ASK YOU... HOW DO YOU— WHAT DO YOU USE...
HOW DO YOU DYE YOUR HAIR?
OOH, ARE YOU GOING TO DYE YOUR HAIR? WHAT COLOR?
I DON'T KNOW, I'M JUST THINKING ABOUT IT.
OHMIGOD, I AM THE **QUEEN** OF HAIR DYE! PLEASE LET ME DO IT! ARE YOU BUSY TODAY? COME OVER TO MY HOUSE AND DO IT TODAY!
LIKE, RIGHT NOW?
TOUGHER. STRONGER. FEARLESS!
... OK!
YES! YOU SKATE HOME, RIGHT? I'M GOING TO SKATE HOME TODAY TOO! I DON'T LIVE THAT FAR, DON'T WORRY. YOU CAN CALL YOUR MOM FROM MY HOUSE.

IT SOUNDS WEIRD TO SAY IT, BUT I COULDN'T REMEMBER THE LAST TIME I'D BEEN TO SOMEONE'S HOUSE BESIDES NICOLE'S.
IT ALSO SOUNDS WEIRD, BUT I SUDDENLY FELT REALLY NERVOUS. I NEVER WORRIED ABOUT WHAT TO SAY AROUND NICOLE. ZOEY WAS SO FRIENDLY AND POPULAR— WHY DID SHE WANT TO HANG OUT WITH ME? WHAT WERE WE GOING TO TALK ABOUT?
LUCKILY, ZOEY TOOK CARE OF MOST OF THE TALKING.
ARE YOU SO EXCITED ABOUT THE BOUT? I CAN'T BELIEVE IT! I HOPE I GET TO PLAY.
I'VE BEEN SKATING WITH ROSEBUDS FOR LIKE THREE MONTHS, BUT I'M STILL NOT VERY GOOD. I HAVEN'T PLAYED IN A BOUT YET.
THE COACHES SAY I NEED TO APPLY MYSELF MORE, BUT I HAVE DRAMA AND STUFF DURING SCHOOL. IT'S NOT LIKE I'LL EVER BE AS GOOD AS HEIDI GO SEEK OR NAPOLEON OR...
OR RAINBOW BITE?
OH MY GOSH, SHE IS A-MA-ZING, ISN'T SHE? SHE IS MY ABSOLUTE FAVORITE!
WE SKATED FOR A WHILE LONGER. I'D NEVER BEEN ON THIS SIDE OF TOWN BEFORE.
OK, IMPORTANT STOP. THE MOST WONDERFUL PLACE ON EARTH, THE PLACE WHERE ALL TEENAGE DREAMS COME TRUE...

Greenwood PHARMACY
?
$3.49
$1.99
CANDY! MAGAZINES! FLIP-FLOPS! STYLISH SUNGLASSES! THIS PLACE IS A MAGICAL WONDERLAND!
AND MOST IMPORTANTLY. . .
5A
HAIR DYE
NOW, YOU DON'T WANT ANYTHING THAT SAYS "NATURAL" OR "EASY" OR "HEALTHY."

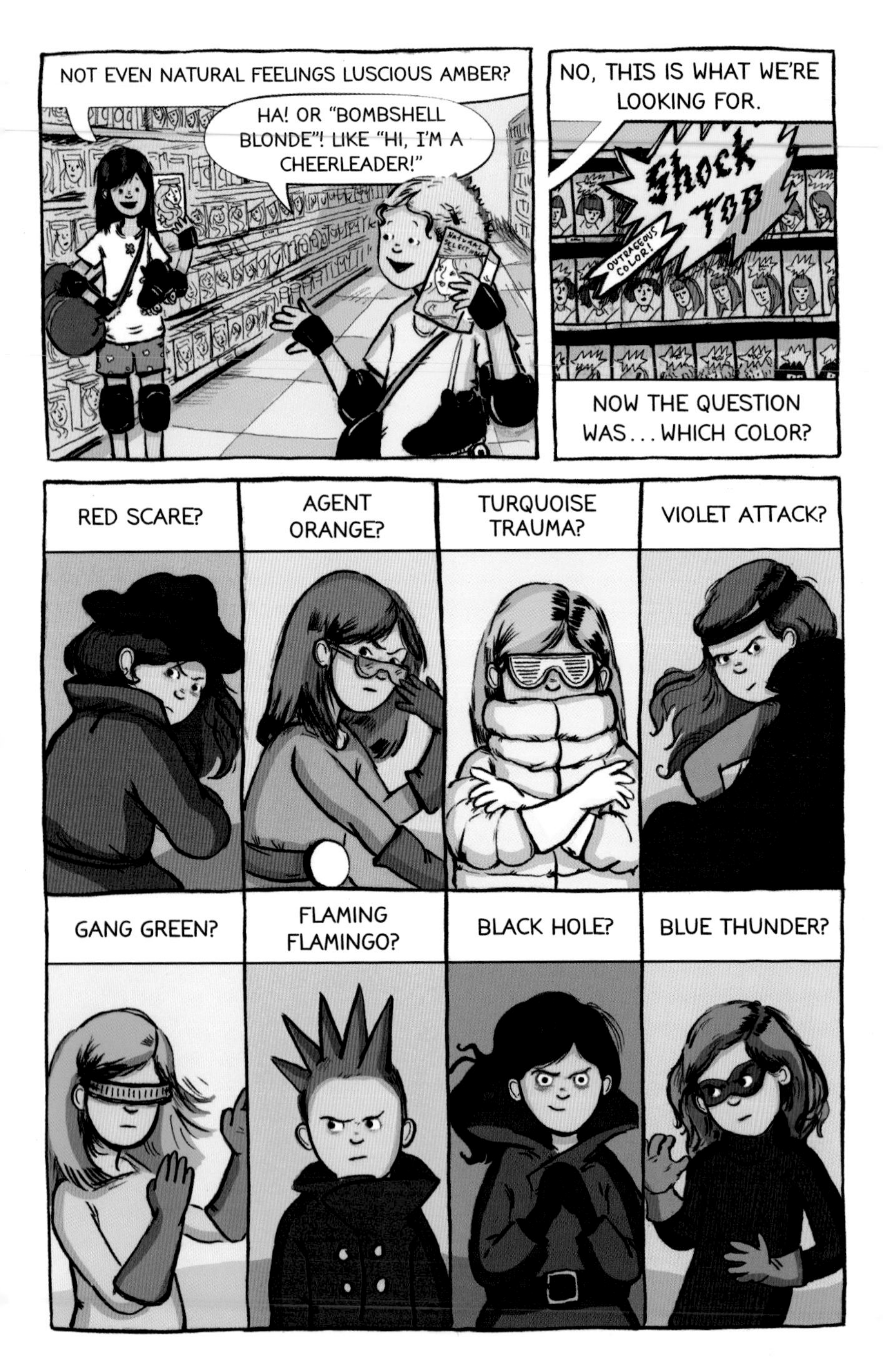
NOT EVEN NATURAL FEELINGS LUSCIOUS AMBER?
HA! OR "BOMBSHELL BLONDE"! LIKE "HI, I'M A CHEERLEADER!"
NATURAL SELECTIONS
NO, THIS IS WHAT WE'RE LOOKING FOR.
Shock Top
OUTRAGEOUS COLOR!
NOW THE QUESTION WAS... WHICH COLOR?
RED SCARE?
AGENT ORANGE?
TURQUOISE TRAUMA?
VIOLET ATTACK?
GANG GREEN?
FLAMING FLAMINGO?
BLACK HOLE?
BLUE THUNDER?

I THINK...I THINK BLUE THUNDER!
EXCELLENT CHOICE! HOW MUCH MONEY DO YOU HAVE?
I HAVE MY $10 EMERGENCY FUND.
HAIR DYE IS **ALWAYS** AN EMERGENCY. I HAVE $7– THAT'S ENOUGH TO PICK UP A FEW NECESSITIES FOR THIS IMPORTANT WORK.
THEY'RE LIFE SAVERS. THEY'RE FOR EMERGENCIES!
LIFE SAVERS
CANDY
CHIPS
SO WHAT'S YOUR MOM GOING TO SAY?
IF SHE DIDN'T WANT ME TO DYE MY HAIR, SHE SHOULDN'T HAVE TAKEN ME TO ROLLER DERBY IN THE FIRST PLACE.
YOUR MOM WON'T MIND THAT I'M OVER? SHE LETS YOU HAVE FRIENDS OVER WHEN YOU'RE HOME ALONE?
OH, WE WON'T BE ALONE. **I AM NEVER ALONE.**

HEY ZOEY, THINK FAST!
UGGHH! IS THIS YOUR SOCK? YOU ARE DISGUSTING.
HEY, WHO'S YOUR FRIEND?
SOMEONE COOL. SO SHE CLEARLY DOESN'T WANT TO MEET YOU.
HEY, ARE THOSE CHIPS IN YOUR BAG?
LET ME HAVE SOME!
GET BACK, YOU TURD BUCKETS! BACK! RUN FOR IT, ASTRID!
TOSS
LIFESAVERS
CANDY

PANT
PANT
ZOEY'S ROOM
SLAM!
WHAT...WHAT WAS THAT?
WELCOME TO MY WORLD. WHAT I WOULDN'T GIVE TO BE AN ONLY CHILD. IT'S LIKE LIVING ON A WILD CHIMPANZEE RESERVE.
WHOA, YOUR ROOM IS AWESOME!
THE PLUS SIDE OF BEING THE ONLY GIRL! I GET THE WHOLE ATTIC TO MYSELF. AND MY OWN BATHROOM.
CATS
OPERA

UM, **THAT'S** A LITTLE CREEPY.
HOW DARE YOU INSULT MY BOYFRIEND LIKE THAT! DON'T LISTEN TO HER, BABY— SOMEDAY WE WILL GO PUBLIC WITH OUR LOVE!
YOUR BOYFRIEND IS WOLVERINE?
MY BOYFRIEND IS HUGH JACKMAN IN *THE BOY FROM OZ*, BUT THEY DON'T MAKE LIFE-SIZED CUTOUTS OF THAT— SO I TAKE WHAT I CAN GET.
OK, LET'S SEE WHAT WE'VE GOT HERE.
CHIPS
DUMP
BLEACH
CONDITIONER PACKET
WHOA.
YOU DON'T NEED THOSE. I KNOW EXACTLY WHAT TO DO.
GRAB
WARNINGS
DIRECTIONS
NOW JUST RELAX, THIS WON'T HURT A BIT.
SNAP

OK, THE FIRST STEP IS BLEACHING, BECAUSE YOUR HAIR IS SO DARK.
BLEACHING? YOU DIDN'T SAY ANYTHING ABOUT **BLEACHING**!
WE **HAVE** TO! IT'S A WASTE OF TIME OTHERWISE– IT WON'T SHOW UP! TRUST ME, I'VE DONE IT HUNDREDS OF TIMES TO MY OWN HAIR.
DO YOU WANT TO DO IT ALL? OR JUST SOME STREAKS?
TOUGHER. STRONGER. FEARLESS.
LET'S GO THE FULL MONTY.
FULL MONTY! THAT'S A MUSICAL! THERE IS HOPE FOR YOU YET!
HERE, PUT THIS TOWEL ON. HOW DO YOU FEEL ABOUT THAT SHIRT? IT MIGHT GET RUINED.
PLEASE RUIN THIS SHIRT.
WAIT! ... AREN'T YOU SUPPOSED TO DO A TEST SECTION FIRST?
I TOLD YOU NOT TO READ THOSE DIRECTIONS.

THIS SMELL IS BURNING MY EYES!
PERFECTLY NATURAL. DON'T WORRY ABOUT IT.
IT SAYS IT CAN TAKE UP TO 60 MINUTES TO BLEACH VERY DARK HAIR.
LET'S WATCH AN INSPIRATIONAL FILM WHILE WE WAIT.
I'VE SEEN THIS MOVIE! MY MOM MADE ME WATCH THIS FOR AN EVENING OF PUERTO RICAN CULTURAL HERITAGE.
OR SOMETHING.
WEST SIDE STORY
ARE YOU FROM PUERTO RICO?
MY MOM IS. WELL, YOU KNOW– LIKE, MY GRANDPARENTS.
CHIPS
YOU'RE SO LUCKY! YOU'RE JUST LIKE MARIA! IT IS MY DREAM TO PLAY ANITA ON BROADWAY ONE DAY.

CATS
YOU'RE REALLY INTO THEATER STUFF, HUH?
YEAH. I'M GOING TO NYU TO STUDY MUSICAL THEATER WHEN I GO TO COLLEGE. AND I WAS IN MY SCHOOL'S PLAY THIS YEAR—*TOM SAWYER*. I WAS ONLY IN THE CHORUS, BUT I HAD ONE SPEAKING LINE. "TO THE CAVES!"
ONLY ONE OTHER 7TH GRADER HAD A SPEAKING PART. MR. BATT LIKES TO GIVE MOST OF THE ROLES TO 8TH AND 9TH GRADERS, SO HOPEFULLY THIS YEAR I'LL GET A BIGGER PART.
HERE'S THE PROGRAM.
Cedar Park Junior High PRESENTS TOM SAWYER THE MUSICAL
I DIDN'T KNOW *TOM SAWYER* WAS A MUSICAL.
LOOK AT TOM SAWYER. BRAD RILEY. ISN'T HE GORGEOUS? LOOK, HE SIGNED MY PROGRAM: "TO THE BEST SUNDAY SCHOOL GIRL #3 EVER SEEN ON STAGE. STAY COOL".
SIGH. TOO BAD HE'S IN HIGH SCHOOL NEXT YEAR. NOT THAT HE COULD EVER TAKE YOUR PLACE, HUGH.

WHAT ABOUT YOU? YOU DO ANY THEATER? WHAT'S YOUR "THING"?
SHE'D BEEN TALKING FOR SO LONG I ALMOST FORGOT TO ANSWER.
CHIPS
MY "THING"?
YOU KNOW, YOUR "THING." WHAT ARE YOU KNOWN AS AT SCHOOL? LIKE, THEY CALL ME "DRAMA GIRL," BECAUSE I'M INTO THEATER. WHAT DO THEY CALL YOU?
I'D ONLY EVER HAD ONE NICKNAME IN SCHOOL, AND IT WASN'T GREAT.
"ASS-TURD."
NO WAY! AH-HA-HA! I'M SORRY, BUT THAT'S SO **MEAN**! WHO COMES UP WITH THIS STUFF?
ONE GUESS WHO CAME UP WITH **THAT** ONE. WHAT KIND OF DEMONIC SECOND GRADER KNOWS THE WORDS "ASS" AND "TURD," ANYWAY?
NOBODY REALLY CALLS ME THAT ANYMORE, NOT SINCE 2ND GRADE. NOW I'M JUST. . . I'M JUST. . . HMMM. . .

IT'S WEIRD, I HAD EVERYONE ELSE IN MY CLASS TOTALLY PEGGED.
SOCCER PLAYER: BRENDAN
CHILD GENIUS: ELEANOR
GEEK: SETH
POPULAR GIRLS/FUTURE CHEERLEADERS OF AMERICA:
SOPHIA
GRACE
ROBERTA
HORSE GIRL: AMY
WEIRDER HORSE GIRL: NATALIE
FUNNY KID: THEO
SUDDENLY, I KNEW WHAT MY "THING" WAS: "NICOLE'S BEST FRIEND."
I GUESS I DON'T HAVE A "THING."
. . . ANYMORE.

WELL, AFTER THIS, THEY'LL CALL YOU "BLUE HAIR GIRL"!
I GUESS. HOW'S IT LOOKING?
HERE'S WHAT HAPPENED TO MY HAIR SO FAR (FROM WHAT I COULD SEE):

IT IS STILL TOTALLY BROWN. YOU MUST HAVE VERY RESISTANT STRANDS. OK, DON'T WORRY— WE JUST NEED TO INCREASE THE FIREPOWER.

SHE PUT ANOTHER HEALTHY SERVING OF BLEACH IN MY HAIR. THEN SHE PUT A SHOWER CAP ON ME, SAYING THE HEAT WOULD MAKE THE BLEACH WORK FASTER.
ALL THIS BLEACH ISN'T GOING TO MAKE MY HAIR FALL OUT, IS IT?
SHE DIDN'T ANSWER, WHICH WASN'T REASSURING.

EVERY 10 MINUTES OR SO SHE'D PEEK IN AND SAY CRYPTIC THINGS LIKE,
OH YES— WE'RE COOKING WITH FIRE NOW!
AT THE MOVIE'S HALFTIME, SHE DECIDED IT HAD BEEN LONG ENOUGH.
ARE YOU READY?
TA-DA!
AAAAAAGH!

OKAY, RELAX, IT'S OK. BREATHE... BUT NOT TOO DEEPLY ON ACCOUNT OF THE FUMES. THIS IS JUST PHASE ONE, OK?
JUST LEAN BACK. YOU'RE EXPERIENCING SOME SHOCK RIGHT NOW, BUT THIS IS NORMAL.
OK, LET'S SIT UP...
SHE WAS SPEAKING TO ME AS IF I WERE A HEAD TRAUMA VICTIM.
AND NOW WE ADD THE BLUE. THIS IS WHERE THINGS GET BETTER.
AHHHHHHH.
IT DID LOOK BETTER– RIGHT AWAY, BECAUSE IT WAS DARK AGAIN.
IT LOOKS THE SAME AS MY REGULAR HAIR!
THAT'S JUST BECAUSE IT'S WET. YOU'LL SEE A DIFFERENCE, TRUST ME. NOW **THIS** ONE WE LET SIT FOR 30 MINUTES.
YOU KNOW WHAT? WHILE WE'RE WAITING, I THINK I'LL ADD A LITTLE PINK STREAK TO MY HAIR.

WHOA, IT'S LIKE YOU HAVE THE WHOLE SHOCK TOP PRODUCT LINE IN THERE!
YEAH, THEY SAY NOT TO SAVE THE LEFTOVER DYE, BUT I ALWAYS DO.
HERE, DO ME UP! JUST MY BANGS.
SO, YOU KNOW, IF YOU PLAY IN THE BOUT, YOU GET TO PICK A DERBY NAME. I'M PRETTY SURE I'M GOING TO GO WITH SLAY MISERABLES— IT'S LIKE MY FAVORITE MUSICAL OF ALL TIME. WHAT'S YOUR NAME GOING TO BE?
I DON'T KNOW— IT'S SUCH A BIG CHOICE.
PICK MY OWN NAME? I WISH I'D BEEN GIVEN THIS CHOICE 12 YEARS AGO. I DON'T KNOW WHY MY MOM CHOSE "ASTRID"— IT'S SO WEIRD. . . . AND IT LETS OTHER KIDS MAKE UP NICKNAMES LIKE "ASS-TURD."
BETTER THINK FAST, YOU'VE ONLY GOT A FEW WEEKS!

FINALLY, AFTER 2 ROUNDS OF "AMERICA" AND 3 ROUNDS OF "I FEEL PRETTY"...
...IT WAS TIME.
IT'S...IT'S SPECTACULAR!
YOU HAVE A LITTLE DYE ON YOUR FOREHEAD & EARS. DON'T WORRY. THAT WILL COME OFF IN 3 OR 4 WEEKS.
I WAS A NEW WOMAN. I WAS GOING TO BE TOUGH! STRONG! FEARLESS!
MY MOM IS GOING TO KILL ME!

DON'T WORRY! SHE'LL GET OVER IT! IT'S NOT LIKE YOU GOT YOUR NOSE PIERCED, OR...
HEYYYYYYYY, **WAIT** A SECOND...
NO.
JUST HEAR ME OUT!
YOU JUST TAKE A PAPERCLIP, BEND IT LIKE SO, AND CUT IT...
VOILA! A FAKE NOSE RING!
MAKE YOUR MOM **REALLY** FREAK, AND THEN BE LIKE, "RELAX, IT'S FAKE!" THEN SHE WON'T FREAK OUT ABOUT YOUR HAIR SO MUCH!
THAT'S...KIND OF A GENIUS IDEA!
THANK YOU, THANK YOU. BUT WAIT, THERE'S MORE...

HEY, MOM. CAN I STAY AT NICOLE'S HOUSE A LITTLE LATER TONIGHT? HER MOM WILL DRIVE ME HOME.
WE STAYED IN THE BATHROOM FOR ANOTHER HOUR.
SLAM!
BANG!
CRASH!
WHEN WE WERE DONE, ZOEY'S 16-YEAR-OLD BROTHER DANNY DROVE ME HOME.
...AND **THAT'S** A RED LIGHT FIRE DRILL!
SO, CAN WE COME IN TO HEAR THE VERBAL BEATDOWN YOU'RE ABOUT TO GET FROM YOUR MOM?
DANNY! QUIT IT, SHE'S NERVOUS ENOUGH!
OK, OK, WE DON'T HAVE TO COME IN. WE'LL PROBABLY HEAR IT FROM OUT HERE ANYWAY.
BYE, ASTRID! SEE YOU TOMORROW. GOOD LUCK!
HERE GOES NOTHING...
1A

ASTRID? IS THAT YOU?
WHY SO MANY LIGHTS, MOM? YOU SHOULD REALLY THINK ABOUT CONSERVING ENERGY.
CLICK
SIGH ASTRID, TURN THAT BACK ON, PLEASE. I'M READING IN HERE.
CLICK
AAAAAAH!
YOUR FACE! YOUR BEAUTIFUL, ANGEL FACE!
MOM. **MOM!** RELAX! THEY'RE FAKE! SEE?
OH, THANK GOODNESS.
MY **HAIR**, ON THE OTHER HAND...
AAAGH!

CHAPTER 9
YOU'RE ALIVE!
I THINK SHE WAS JUST HAPPY I DIDN'T GET A TATTOO. AND SHE SAID I HAVE TO DYE MY HAIR BACK BEFORE SCHOOL STARTS– SHE DOESN'T WANT TEACHERS GETTING THE "WRONG IDEA," WHATEVER THAT MEANS.
THE WRONG IDEA, LIKE, YOU'RE AWESOME?
I KNOW! I THINK IT SENDS EXACTLY THE **RIGHT** IDEA!
TWEET TWEET!
LADIES, LISTEN UP! YESTERDAY DURING THE HITTING DRILLS I DIDN'T SEE A LOT OF FIRE GOING ON.
WHEN YOU'RE PLAYING ROLLER DERBY, YOU NEED TO BE FIERCE! YOU MAY BE FRIENDS WITH EVERYBODY OFF THE TRACK, BUT ON THE TRACK? THEY ARE NOT YOUR FRIENDS.
THIS DRILL IS CALLED "WARFACE."

NOW, GET INTO A PACELINE...
HA! I'M NOT GETTING IN FRONT **THIS** TIME!
THE FIRST PERSON WORKS THEIR WAY UP, BACK TO FRONT. THAT MEANS YOU'RE FIRST, ASTRID.
RATS!
YOU'RE GOING TO WEAVE THROUGH THE LINE. WHEN YOU COME UP NEXT TO SOMEONE,
I WANT YOU TO LOOK YOUR OPPONENT IN THE EYE AND SHOW THEM YOUR WARFACE. LIKE THIS...
RRRRRGH!
SWOOSH
RRRRRGH!
SWOOSH
RRRRRGH!
SWOOSH

OK, EVERYONE START SKATING!
ASTRID, ON THE WHISTLE...
TWEET!
RRRRGGGH! (*GIGGLE*)
SWOOSH
RRRRGGGH! (*GIGGLE*)
SWOOSH
RRRRGGGH! (*GIGGLE*)
SWOOSH
TWEET TWEET!
HOLD UP. ASTRID, YOU CALL THAT A **WARFACE**?! THAT WOULDN'T SCARE A PUPPY.
LADIES, THIS IS NOT A JOKE. WHEN YOU PLAY ROLLER DERBY, YOU LEAVE IT ALL ON THE TRACK. YOU CAN'T HOLD BACK, OR BE EMBARRASED, OR SELF-CONSCIOUS. I WANT YOU TO SHOW ME THE FIRE, OR GO HOME.

ASTRID, SHOW ME YOUR WARFACE.
ARRRRGGH?
SHOW ME YOUR WARFACE!
AAARRRRRGH!
IS THAT ALL YOU CAN DO?!? SHOW ME YOUR WARFACE!!

AAAGH

NOW GO GET 'EM!

AAAAAAAAAAAARRRRRGHH!!!

FEEL THE DIFFERENCE?
PANT
PANT
WARFACE IS EXHAUSTING!
IT FEELS... GOOD!
I HAD A NEW QUESTION FOR RAINBOW BITE AFTER PRACTICE.
Dear Rainbow Bite,
Thank you for your note. I am trying to be stronger and fearless. Do you have any tips for putting your warface on?
Your biggest fan,
Rose Dud
Rainbow Bite
SHOVE

MY ANSWER CAME THE VERY NEXT DAY.
Dear Dud,
Tip of the day: When you're hitting someone, imagine you're hitting your worst enemy on the planet.
That is all, Bitey
WELL, **THAT** SHOULD MAKE HITTING PRACTICE WAY MORE FUN!
TAKE THAT, RACHEL!
BAM!
TWEET TWEET!
LADIES! TAKE A SEAT! IN PREPARATION FOR THE BOUT, TODAY WE ARE GOING TO TALK ABOUT GAME PLAY!
AS MOST OF YOU KNOW, THIS...
...IS A PANTY!

PANTY! HEE HEE!
THE JAMMER PANTY HAS A STAR ON IT.
THE PIVOT PANTY HAS A STRIPE.
YOU PUT THESE ON OVER YOUR HELMET. LIKE SO.
WHO CAN TELL ME WHAT THE PIVOT DOES?
SHE'S LIKE, HEAD BLOCKER. YOU KNOW, LIKE HEAD BOY AND HEAD GIRL IN HARRY POTTER. SHE TELLS YOU WHERE TO LINE UP AND STUFF.

CLOSE ENOUGH. OK, WHO WANTS TO BE PIVOT IN THIS SCENARIO? BRAIDY, HERE YOU GO.
OK, I NEED 3 MORE BLOCKERS ON THE TRACK.
NOW THE JAMMER. WHAT DOES SHE DO?
SHE'S THE ONE WHO SCORES THE POINTS!
YES. SHE'S THE **ONLY** ONE WHO CAN SCORE POINTS, AND SHE DOES SO BY GETTING PAST THE BLOCKERS.
WHO WANTS TO BE JAMMER?
THRILLA, COME ON UP.
HMMPH.

OK, IN THIS SCENARIO, WE HAVE A POOR JAMMER WITH NO TEAMMATES ON THE TRACK. SHE'S ALL ALONE. THE BLOCKERS LINE UP ON THE TRACK AS A WALL...
AND THE JAMMER LINES UP BEHIND THEM, ON THE JAMMER LINE.
THE BLOCKERS ARE TRYING TO **STOP** THE JAMMER.
THE JAMMER WANTS TO GET PAST THE BLOCKERS. SIMPLE ENOUGH, RIGHT?
WHEN I BLOW THE WHISTLE,
TWEET!
EVERYONE STARTS.
HEIDI STARTED TALKING ABOUT ALL SORTS OF STRATEGY, USING WORDS LIKE "OFFENSE" AND "DEFENSE" AND "WALLS"...
...BUT I WASN'T REALLY LISTENING.

THE JAMMER WAS OBVIOUSLY THE MOST IMPORTANT PLAYER.
SHE HAD TO BE FAST.
AND WILY.
SHE WAS THE STAR—JUST LIKE RAINBOW BITE.
THAT IS WHAT I WANT TO DO!
UNFORTUNATELY...
GULP

...JAMMING TURNED OUT TO BE A LITTLE HARDER THAN IT LOOKED.
BAM!
HEIDI HAD HER CLIPBOARD OUT THE ENTIRE WEEK, AND THIS MADE ME NERVOUS. WAS SHE TAKING NOTES ON MY SKATING? WAS SHE DECIDING IF I'D GET TO PLAY IN THE BOUT OR NOT?
I STARTED PULLING OUT MY TRIED & TRUE TRICKS OF GETTING MOM IN A GOOD MOOD WHEN I WANTED SOMETHING.
YOUR DREADLOCKS ARE LOOKING BEAUTIFUL TODAY, HEIDI!
OOOH, NEW TATTOO, HEIDI?
UNDER YOUR TUTELAGE, HEIDI, I THINK I AM REALLY BEGINNING TO BLOSSOM!
I DON'T KNOW IF SHE WAS BUYING IT OR NOT.

IT DIDN'T STOP ME FROM TRYING— LIKE ON FRIDAY, WHEN SHE ASKED FOR VOLUNTEERS TO HAND OUT FLYERS FOR THE UPCOMING BOUT.
I NEED A FEW OF YOU TO COME TO OAKS PARK TONIGHT FROM 5 TO 7. IT'S FAMILY FUN NIGHT, AND IT WOULD BE A GREAT PLACE TO HAND OUT FLYERS AND TALK TO PEOPLE ABOUT ROLLER DERBY.
I'LL DO IT, HEIDI!
FRIENDLY, HELPFUL, TEAM-PLAYER SMILE.
OOOKAYYYY... THANKS, ASTRID!
I CAN COME WITH YOU!
COOL! YOU CAN COME OVER TO MY HOUSE FOR DINNER IF YOU WANT!
SO, ZOEY SKATED HOME WITH ME AFTER CAMP. I MADE MY USUAL STOP.
E-Z STOP
MY BEST CUSTOMER! SURE, YOU CAN PUT A FLYER IN THE WINDOW!
ROLLER DERBY

SOMETHING CAUGHT MY EYE AS I WAS HANGING UP MY FLYER...
ROLLER DERBY
FANCY THAT— NICOLE'S DANCE CAMP WAS HAVING A RECITAL THE WEEK AFTER OUR BOUT.
Northwest Dance Academy
Summer Recital
July 30th, 7 pm
ROLLER DERBY
TECHNICALLY, I'M NOT ALLOWED TO HAVE FRIENDS OVER WHEN MOM'S NOT HOME... SO WE HAD TO DO A LITTLE WORK-AROUND.
!
?
MOM! I'M HOME!
1A
CAN ZOEY STAY FOR DINNER?

CALL ME IF ZOEY'S PARENTS CAN'T PICK YOU UP AFTER ALL. DON'T TALK TO ANY STRANGERS.
MOM, IT'S STILL LIGHT OUT.
THANKS FOR DINNER, MRS. V.
IT WAS NICE MEETING YOU, ZOEY... EVEN IF YOU ARE THE ONE RESPONSIBLE FOR ASTRID'S HAIR.
BEEP BEEP!
YES!
FIRST THINGS FIRST, WE NEEDED TO RESTORE OUR ENERGY FOR THE IMPORTANT WORK AHEAD.
SODA $3
ZOEY WAS CRAZY— SHE'D SHOUT ANYTHING TO PEOPLE WALKING BY.
I LIKE YOUR SHIRT!
I LIKE YOUR HAIR!
DO YOU LIKE HAVING FUN? IF YOU LIKE HAVING FUN, YOU'LL **LOVE** ROLLER DERBY!

WE SETTLED NEAR THE GAME OF STRENGTH, AND ZOEY STARTED SHOUTING LIKE A CARNIVAL BARKER.
ROLLER DERBY! STEP RIGHT UP! GET YOUR ROLLER DERBY FLYERS RIGHT HERE!
STOP! MY STOMACH!
WAIT, I HAVE AN IDEA.
LICK
ROLLER DERBY
COME SEE THE AMAZING FORTUNE TELLER! SHE SEES THE FUTURE!
WHAT DID YOU SAY?
I SEE. . .ROLLER DERBY IN YOUR FUTURE!
ROLLER DERBY?! I SEE A NUTHOUSE IN YOUR FUTURE!

HA
HA
HA
HA
HA
STOP LAUGHING! I SEE A NUTHOUSE IN **YOUR** FUTURE!
ROLLER DERBY
FORTUNES! ROLLER DERBY FORTUNES! STEP RIGHT UP!
I CAN SEEEEE THE FUTURE!
ROLLER DERBY
BON
ASTRID?
I'D KNOW THAT VOICE ANYWHERE... I'D HEARD IT NEARLY EVERY DAY FOR THE PAST FIVE YEARS. MAYBE I REALLY **COULD** SEE THE FUTURE, BECAUSE WITH MY EYES CLOSED I SAID:
ROLLER DERBY
NICOLE?

I HADN'T SEEN HER FOR WEEKS— NOT SINCE THAT DAY IN FRONT OF HER HOUSE. AND HERE SHE WAS . . . WITH RACHEL, ADAM, AND KEITH.

I FELT SO WEIRD. I WAS SHOCKED TO SEE HER OUT OF THE BLUE LIKE THIS, AND PART OF ME FELT KIND OF SICK. . . . BUT THE OTHER PART OF ME WAS STILL ON A FRANTIC SUGAR-LAUGHING HIGH.

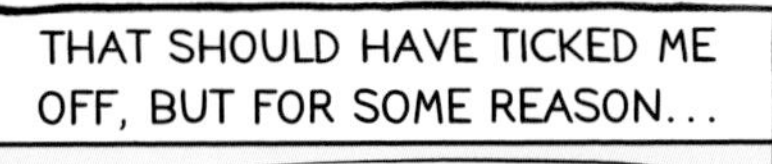

WEIRDO.
MAY I OFFER YOU A FLYER?
ROLLER DERBY?
YOU PLAY ROLLER DERBY?
NO WAY!
SO DO YOU, LIKE, BEAT EACH OTHER UP?
SHUT UP—SHE PLAYS ROLLER DERBY. SHE COULD BEAT **YOU** UP!
I ONLY USE MY POWERS FOR GOOD, NOT EVIL.
NICOLE KEPT STARING AT ME. I COULDN'T HELP STARING AT HER, EITHER.
WAS SHE ON A **DATE** WITH ADAM? I DON'T KNOW WHY THIS MADE ME FEEL SO WEIRD... BUT IT DID.
COME ON! WE HAVE TO MEET MY MOM IN AN HOUR. LET'S GO!
LITTERING IS A CRIME!
UGH. FRIENDS OF YOURS?
ROLLER DERB

...NO.
WATCHING NICOLE WALK AWAY, I FELT A SORT OF SICK FASCINATION.
WAS SHE GOING TO HOLD HANDS WITH ADAM? WAS SHE GOING TO **KISS** HIM?
HEY, LET'S FOLLOW THEM!
NAN
WHAT FOR? THEY SEEM LIKE LOSERS.
IT'LL BE FUNNY! COME ON— WE CAN MAKE FUN OF THEM!
I GUESS. WE'RE ALMOST OUT OF FLYERS ANYWAY.
HEY, YOU WANT TO RIDE THE LOG FLUME?
HEY, WAIT UP!

WE FOLLOWED THEM FOR A LITTLE BIT— NOTHING TOO INTERESTING HAPPENED. MOSTLY NICOLE & RACHEL GIGGLED, AND ADAM & KEITH PUNCHED EACH OTHER.
THEY TALKED ABOUT THE STUPIDEST THINGS.
"IS MY LIP GLOSS OK? EWW, I LIKE TOTALLY CHIPPED A NAIL. EWW, IT'S SO DIRTY HERE."
SHE IS SO ANNOYING! WHY DOES ANYONE PUT UP WITH HER?
CAN YOU BOYS GET US SOME DIET COKES? I HAVE TO TALK TO NICOLE. **ALONE.**
THERE. PERFECT. NOW WE'RE GOING TO RIDE THE FERRIS WHEEL, AND ADAM WILL **HAVE** TO KISS YOU THEN. IT'S PRACTICALLY WHY FERRIS WHEELS WERE INVENTED.
ARE YOU SURE? HE HASN'T TRIED TO HOLD MY HAND OR ANYTHING.
TRUST ME.
UNLESS, OF COURSE, THAT FREAK SHOW ASTRID SCARED HIM OFF. I CAN'T BELIEVE YOU USED TO BE FRIENDS WITH HER.

MY HEART STOPPED BEATING, AND THAT SODA WASN'T TASTING SO GOOD ANYMORE.
SHE'S SO... DIFFERENT NOW. I DON'T KNOW WHAT HAPPENED.
SHE'S PROBABLY ON DRUGS OR SOMETHING.
DRUGS!! WHAT WAS THIS GIRL'S PROBLEM?! HAD SHE LOST ALL GRIP ON REALITY?
I DON'T THINK SHE'S ON DRUGS.
WHATEVER. ALL I KNOW IS, YOU DON'T WANT TO GET A BAD REPUTATION ON THE FIRST DAY OF JUNIOR HIGH.
JUST BECAUSE YOU WERE FRIENDS LAST YEAR, DOESN'T MEAN YOU HAVE TO BE FRIENDS THIS YEAR.
HOW DO YOU JUST STOP BEING FRIENDS WITH SOMEBODY?
WHAT'S WEIRD IS... THIS WAS THE SAME EXACT QUESTION I'D BEEN ASKING MYSELF FOR THE PAST FEW WEEKS. MAYBE IT'S ONE OF THOSE GREAT MYSTERIES OF THE UNIVERSE.

...UNLESS YOU'RE THE SPAWN OF THE DEVIL, OF COURSE. **THEN** YOU HAVE AN ANSWER.
THE BEST THING TO DO IS JUST STOP TALKING TO HER. COLD TURKEY.
MY HEART STARTED THUMPING AGAINST MY RIB CAGE.
IT SOUNDS MEAN, BUT IT'S MEANER TO STRING HER ALONG AND PRETEND YOU'RE STILL FRIENDS.
NICOLE WASN'T GOING TO GO ALONG WITH THIS, WAS SHE?
IF SHE SAYS HI TO YOU IN THE HALLS, JUST IGNORE HER.
I WAITED FOR NICOLE TO TELL HER TO STUFF IT. THAT IT WAS A MEAN AND HATEFUL THING TO DO TO ANOTHER PERSON.

WHAT SHE SAID WAS:
I GUESS SO.
I FELT LIKE A ZOMBIE HAD TAKEN OVER MY BRAIN. I COULD BARELY SEE AS I CAME AROUND THE TREE.
ASTRID!
I JUST WANT TO TELL YOU, YOU DON'T HAVE TO WORRY. I WON'T SAY HI TO YOU AT SCHOOL. I'LL NEVER SAY ANOTHER WORD TO YOU AGAIN!
I DIDN'T WANT TO HURT YOUR FEELINGS...
WHO WANTS TO HANG OUT WITH YOU ANYWAY? YOU'RE BORING! AND SHALLOW! SOME PEOPLE CARE ABOUT MORE THAN LIPSTICK, AND CLOTHES, AND BOYS!

YOU OBVIOUSLY CARE ABOUT NONE OF THOSE THINGS. NOW WHY DON'T YOU AND YOUR GIRLFRIEND GO CRAWL BACK UNDER A ROCK AND LEAVE US ALONE.
OUT OF NOWHERE, IT CAME.
WAR FACE!
AAAAAAGH!
I DON'T KNOW WHY I DID IT. I DIDN'T MEAN TO HIT THEM—I JUST MEANT TO THROW MY SODA AT THEIR FEET. BUT A FUNNY THING ABOUT PHYSICS...
Velocity
+
Gravity
70°
Outward
Propulsion
Point of Impact

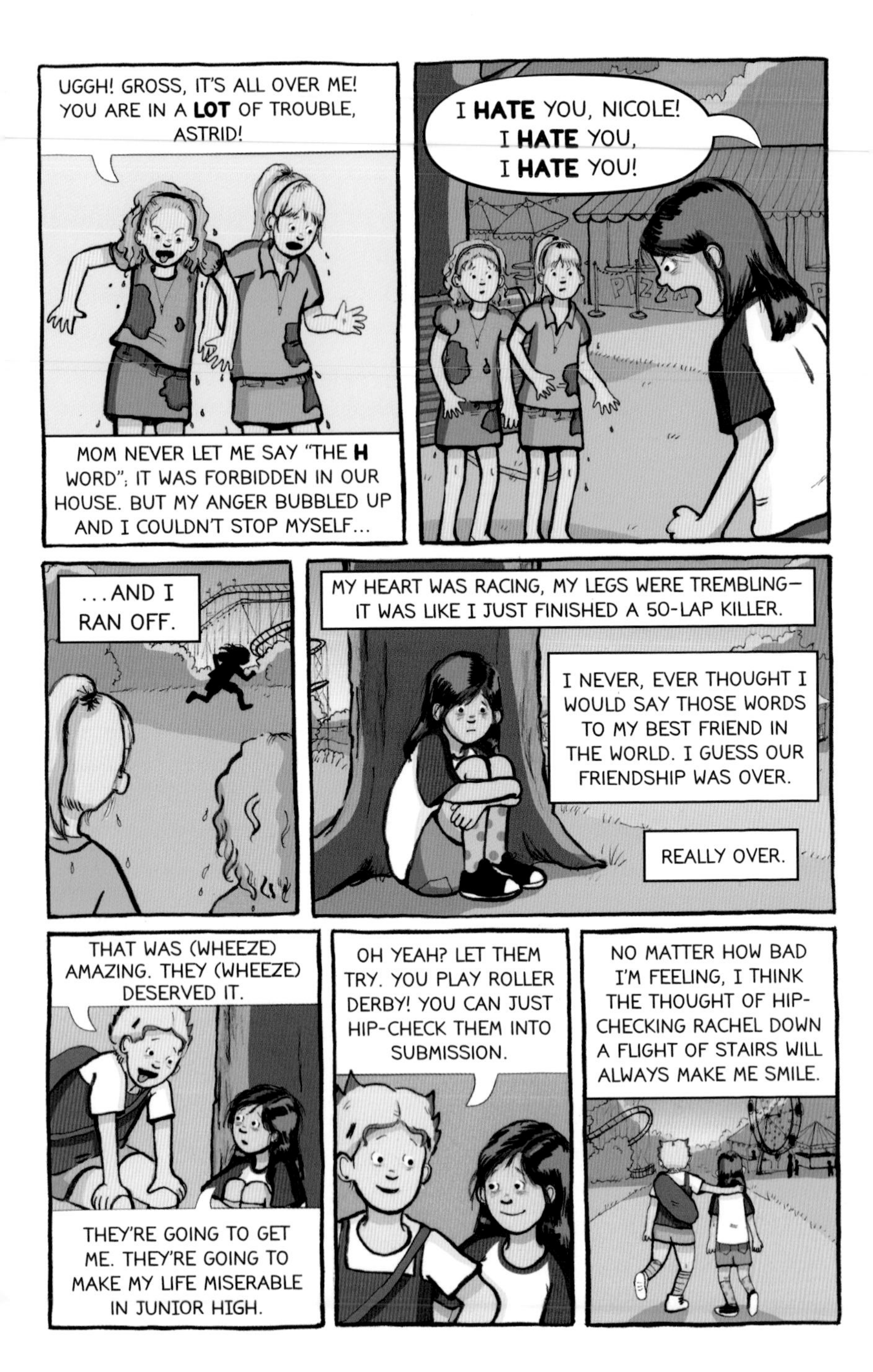
UGGH! GROSS, IT'S ALL OVER ME! YOU ARE IN A LOT OF TROUBLE, ASTRID!
MOM NEVER LET ME SAY "THE H WORD"; IT WAS FORBIDDEN IN OUR HOUSE. BUT MY ANGER BUBBLED UP AND I COULDN'T STOP MYSELF...
I HATE YOU, NICOLE! I HATE YOU, I HATE YOU!
PIZZA
...AND I RAN OFF.
MY HEART WAS RACING, MY LEGS WERE TREMBLING— IT WAS LIKE I JUST FINISHED A 50-LAP KILLER.
I NEVER, EVER THOUGHT I WOULD SAY THOSE WORDS TO MY BEST FRIEND IN THE WORLD. I GUESS OUR FRIENDSHIP WAS OVER.
REALLY OVER.
THAT WAS (WHEEZE) AMAZING. THEY (WHEEZE) DESERVED IT.
THEY'RE GOING TO GET ME. THEY'RE GOING TO MAKE MY LIFE MISERABLE IN JUNIOR HIGH.
OH YEAH? LET THEM TRY. YOU PLAY ROLLER DERBY! YOU CAN JUST HIP-CHECK THEM INTO SUBMISSION.
NO MATTER HOW BAD I'M FEELING, I THINK THE THOUGHT OF HIP-CHECKING RACHEL DOWN A FLIGHT OF STAIRS WILL ALWAYS MAKE ME SMILE.

CHAPTER 10
I THOUGHT I WANTED TO PLAY IN THAT BOUT BEFORE...BUT SOMETHING CHANGED IN ME AFTER MY RUN-IN WITH NICOLE AND RACHEL. NOW I **NEEDED** TO PLAY IN THAT BOUT.
I CAN'T REALLY EXPLAIN THE FIRE THAT CAME OVER ME. I'D NEVER BEEN SO MAD BEFORE, AND I LET THE MAD RUN THROUGH MY VEINS LIKE ROCKET FUEL. I WAS A WOMAN POSSESSED.
IT'S LIKE I PUT MY WARFACE ON, AND I COULDN'T TAKE IT OFF.
I PRACTICED MY HIP CHECKS IN THE DOORWAY.
TAKE THAT, RACHEL!
BAM!
BAM!
TAKE THAT, NICOLE!
I GOT BRUISES ON MY HIPS AND ARMS, AND THEY FELT GOOD.

I DID LUNGES WHILE DOING MY CHORES,
SQUATS WHILE WATCHING TV.
WHAT I **REALLY** WANTED TO DO WAS GO SUPER-FAST— BUT THE HALLWAY WASN'T LONG ENOUGH TO BUILD UP ANY REAL SPEED.
SLAM!
OW.
ARE YOU SURE YOU DON'T NEED A BREAK? YOU'VE BEEN GOING AT THIS AWFULLY HARD.
GRUNT
MOM, I **HAVE** TO WORK HARD. I REALLY WANT THIS.
JUST... DON'T GO OVERBOARD. OKAY?
GRUNT

I BROUGHT THE FIRE TO PRACTICE ON MONDAY.
JUNIOR HIGH
ASTRID? DRILL'S OVER— YOU CAN STOP NOW.
I SOUGHT SOME ADVICE FROM THE EXPERTS.
Dear Rainbow,
I really want to be a jammer in the Rosebuds bout, but I'm worried I'm not good enough. Any advice?
-Dud
Dud-
I've found if you want something badly enough, you just have to work harder than everyone else to get it.
-Bitey
WORK HARDER THAN EVERYONE ELSE? I CAN DO THAT.

WANT TO COME OVER TODAY? I RENTED A DVD OF XANADU! GET THIS... IT'S A MUSICAL...ON ROLLER SKATES!
ACTUALLY—I THINK I WANT TO STAY AND PRACTICE A LITTLE MORE.
WHAT? WE JUST HAD PRACTICE FOR THREE HOURS!
I WANT TO SKATE IN THIS BOUT. DON'T YOU?
YEAH, BUT... XANADU!
YOU CAN'T STAY HERE IN THE HANGAR WITHOUT ADULT SUPERVISION... BUT I HAVE SOME PAPERWORK TO TAKE CARE OF, SO I'LL BE HERE FOR ANOTHER HOUR OR SO. YOUR PARENTS KNOW ABOUT THIS?
OH YES, WE CALLED! THEY SAID IT'S FINE.
OW!

MAYBE YOU'RE WONDERING ABOUT THE STATE OF MY SKATING NOW.
READY, SET...
...GO!
I'M PRETTY FAST NOW!
I WIN!
STOPPING IS STILL NOT MY STRONG SUIT.
OW.
BUT WHO NEEDS TO STOP WHEN YOU CAN GO FAST?
MY HITTING'S GETTING BETTER—SORT OF.
YOU ALMOST MOVED ME THAT TIME!

AND WHEN I **GET** HIT, I ONLY FALL ABOUT 80% OF THE TIME.
THUNK
OK, 90%
THUNK
95%
THUNK
THAT'S OK, BECAUSE I DON'T WANT TO BE A BLOCKER. I'M GOING TO BE A JAMMER, AND I'LL BE SO FAST THAT NO ONE WILL BE ABLE TO HIT ME!
THREE CHEERS FOR ASTRID!
AND WITH AN AMAZING 25-POINT JAM, ASTRID WINS THE GAME!
SHE'S GOING TO BE, LIKE, THE COOLEST GIRL IN JUNIOR HIGH.
WHY DID I EVER DITCH HER? WHAT HAVE I DONE?

ZOEY AND I PRACTICED AS OFTEN AS WE COULD AFTER CAMP.
OK LADIES! PACK IT UP, I'M GETTING OUT OF HERE.
I'M REALLY IMPRESSED WITH ALL THE EXTRA SKATING YOU GIRLS HAVE BEEN DOING. I'VE SEEN A LOT OF IMPROVEMENT, AND NAPOLEON HAS NOTICED IT TOO.
ARE WE GOOD ENOUGH TO PLAY IN THE BOUT?
I'D SAY THERE'S A GOOD CHANCE!
YES!
I DIDN'T LET UP.
AM I GOOD ENOUGH TO BE A **JAMMER**?
I CAN'T MAKE ANY PROMISES. FOR A SHORT GAME LIKE THIS, WE'LL PROBABLY HAVE THE MORE EXPERIENCED GIRLS JAMMING, SINCE WE HAVEN'T HAD MUCH TIME FOR TRAINING.
BUT SAY IF SOMEONE PRACTICES **REALLY** HARD? AND GETS A LOT BETTER? **THEN** COULD THEY BE A JAMMER?
LIKE I SAID, NO PROMISES. BUT YOU'RE BOTH DOING GREAT, SO KEEP UP THE GOOD WORK.

DID YOU HEAR THAT? WE'RE IN THE BOUT! WE GET TO PLAY! I HOPE WE'RE ON THE SAME TEAM!
HEY, DO YOU WANT TO COME OVER TOMORROW? WE CAN WORK ON OUR LISTS OF DERBY NAMES. WE CAN DECORATE OUR HELMETS! **WE CAN WATCH XANADU!**
THANKS BUT— I THINK I'M GOING TO PRACTICE AGAIN TOMORROW.
WHAT?! BUT YOU JUST HEARD HER— WE'RE IN THE BOUT!
YEAH, BUT I WANT TO BE A **JAMMER**.
YOU'RE NUTS. RELAX A LITTLE, GIRLFRIEND! HAVE SOME FUN!
IF YOU WANT SOMETHING BAD ENOUGH, YOU HAVE TO WORK HARDER THAN EVERYONE ELSE.
ARE YOU ONE OF THOSE KIDS IN SCHOOL WITH LIKE A 4.7 GPA?
SEE YOU TOMORROW, ZOEY.

NOBODY ELSE SEEMED TO BE TAKING PRACTICE ALL THAT SERIOUSLY.
I DID SIT-UPS DURING THE DAILY 10:15 DANCE PARTY BREAK.
C'MON GUYS, QUIT GOOFING AROUND.
ASTRID? YOU SURE YOU DON'T WANT TO COME OVER? LEARN SOME HOT SKATING MOVES FROM OLIVIA NEWTON-JOHN HERSELF?
NO, I'M GOING TO STAY AND WORK ON MY CROSSOVERS.
IT'S NOT AS MUCH FUN TO PRACTICE BY YOURSELF, THAT'S FOR SURE. BUT THIS WASN'T ABOUT HAVING FUN— THIS WAS ABOUT JAMMING IN THAT BOUT.

THINGS GOT EVEN MORE SERIOUS AT THE END OF THE WEEK.
OK! WE'RE NOW 2 WEEKS AWAY FROM THE BOUT, SO WE'RE GOING TO SPLIT YOU INTO YOUR TEAMS!
AFTER MUCH DISCUSSION, NAPOLEON AND I HAVE DECIDED THAT ALL OF YOU CAN PLAY! YOU'VE ALL MADE A LOT OF PROGRESS, SO CONGRATULATIONS!
YAY!
YES!
BRAIDY PUNCH, TOXIC, THRILLA GODZILLA, MARZ ROLLVER, AND SCREAM SODA.... YOU LADIES ARE ON TEAM A. NAPEOLEON WILL BE YOUR BENCH COACH.
THE REST OF YOU ARE TEAM B WITH ME.
YES! WE'RE ON THE SAME TEAM!

HAVE A SEAT, WE HAVE A FEW THINGS TO TALK ABOUT.
WHAT ABOUT POSITIONS?
ANY QUESTIONS?
WHAT ABOUT POSITIONS?
GOOD QUESTION. SINCE WE DIDN'T HAVE MUCH TIME FOR TRAINING, WE'RE ONLY GOING TO HAVE 3 JAMMERS PER TEAM. IF YOU'RE NOT CHOSEN, DON'T WORRY— YOU'LL GET YOUR CHANCE IN THE FUTURE. OK?
TEAM A, YOUR JAMMERS WILL BE, THRILLA GODZILLA, MARZ ROLLVER, AND SCREAM SODA.
YAY!
YES!

ZOEY. YOU'RE JAMMER NUMBER THREE.

ME?! HAVE YOU SEEN ME JAM?
DON'T WORRY— YOU'LL BE GREAT!
IF YOU WANTED TO JAM AND YOU WEREN'T CHOSEN, PLEASE DON'T BE DISAPPOINTED. THIS IS A SHORT BOUT, AND YOU WILL GET YOUR CHANCE IN THE FUTURE. OK, GET TOGETHER WITH YOUR TEAM BY THE BENCHES.
I CAN'T BELIEVE IT! I WAS SURE THEY'D PICK YOU INSTEAD OF ME!
YOU DON'T EVEN **WANT** TO BE A JAMMER!
YEAH, I KNOW, BUT... IT'S PRETTY COOL THAT THEY PICKED ME! I ALWAYS THOUGHT I WAS TERRIBLE AT JAMMING!
IF YOU DON'T WANT TO DO IT, YOU SHOULD TELL THEM. YOU SHOULDN'T HAVE TO DO IT IF YOU DON'T WANT TO.
LOOK, I'M SORRY. BUT AT LEAST YOU GET TO PLAY! AND YOU'RE GETTING SO MUCH BETTER, YOU'LL BE JAMMING IN NO TIME!
I KNOW, IT'S JUST... I CAN'T...
I COULDN'T EXPLAIN MY DISAPPOINTMENT TO HER. BUT SOMEHOW... IT FELT LIKE NICOLE AND RACHEL HAD WON, AND I HAD LOST.

YOU COULD BE **HAPPY** FOR ME.
I **AM** HAPPY FOR YOU, IT'S JUST...
I WOULD HAVE BEEN HAPPY FOR YOU, YOU KNOW.
AND I KNOW SHE WOULD HAVE BEEN. THAT MADE ME FEEL EVEN WORSE.
ASTRID, I KNOW YOU WANTED TO JAM IN THIS BOUT. AND YOU'LL GET THERE! BUT WE NEED YOU TO WORK ON YOUR TEAMWORK FOR NOW. OK?
SNIFF
NOD
PRACTICE DIDN'T GET ANY BETTER AFTER THAT. WHEN IT WAS TIME TO LEAVE, ZOEY WOULDN'T EVEN LOOK AT ME.
WHAT'S THAT? YOU DON'T BELIEVE THE WORST DAY OF MY LIFE COULD **GET** ANY WORSE?
I WOULDN'T HAVE BELIEVED IT EITHER... UNTIL MOM CAME HOME FROM WORK.
OK, GET IN THE CAR!
WE'RE GOING CLOTHES SHOPPING!

CHAPTER • 11
Young Misses
NOOOOOOOOO!
THIS LOOKS CUTE!
TRY THIS ON!

DRESSING ROOM
EARTH TO ASTRID! COME ON OUT— YOU'VE BEEN IN THERE FOR FIVE MINUTES!
DRESSING ROOM
THIS ONE IS A **NO**.
COME OUT ANYWAY, I WANT TO SEE IT.
OH, IT'S...
THIS IS THE MOST HIDEOUS DRESS I'VE EVER SEEN, AND I THINK IT'S GIVING ME A RASH. CAN I PLEASE TAKE THIS OFF NOW?
NICOLE!
MOM! I FORGOT...
...AND FOR ONCE IN MY RECENT STRING OF LIES, MY MIND WAS A COMPLETE BLANK. I COULD THINK OF NOTHING TO DIVERT MY MOM'S ATTENTION.
NICOLE! OVER HERE, SWEETIE!

OH MY GOODNESS, IT'S SO NICE TO SEE YOU! I HAVEN'T SEEN YOU IN WEEKS!
YOU KNOW THAT SAYING "A DEER IN HEADLIGHTS"?
YOU TELL HER, NICOLE. ISN'T THAT DRESS CUTE?
IT'S CUTE, I GUESS.
SIGH IT'S THE HAIR. NOTHING GOES WITH THAT HAIR. HOW DID YOU ESCAPE THE HAIR DYEING?
I THINK MY MOM WOULD KILL ME IF I DYED MY HAIR.
DIDN'T STOP ASTRID. SO, ARE YOU EXCITED ABOUT THE BOUT? IT'S ALL ASTRID TALKS ABOUT. SHE SAYS YOU'RE REALLY DOING WELL AT SKATE CAMP!
SKATE CAMP?
THIS WAS IT. MY COVER WAS BLOWN. I COULD SEE CONFUSION WRITTEN ALL OVER NICOLE'S FACE.
THE ROLLER DERBY SKATE CAMP? THE ONE YOU AND ASTRID HAVE BEEN ATTENDING FOR THE PAST THREE WEEKS?
NICOLE LOOKED FROM MOM —TO ME—TO MOM. I SAW HER CONFUSION CHANGE TO UNDERSTANDING. AND I KNEW SHE WAS ABOUT TO GET HER ULTIMATE REVENGE.
?

YOU DIDN'T TELL HER?
OH MAN.
TELL ME WHAT?
FUNNY STORY, MOM, IT TURNS OUT NICOLE...
IT TURNS OUT... I'M GOING TO BE OUT OF TOWN FOR THE BOUT.
OH, WELL, THAT'S TOO BAD. I KNOW IT'S SUPPOSED TO BE A HIGHLIGHT OF THE CAMP.
RELIEF FLOODED THROUGH ME...AND I ACTUALLY SHOT NICOLE A SMALL SMILE, BEFORE I REMEMBERED YOU DON'T SMILE AT YOUR ENEMIES.
IS YOUR MOM HERE WITH YOU? I'VE BEEN MEANING TO TALK TO HER ABOUT THE CARPOOLING, MAKE SURE EVERYTHING'S OK...
ACTUALLY, I'M WITH MY DAD. I'M SUPPOSED TO MEET HIM OVER IN HOUSEWARES. I FORGOT.
BYE, ASTRID. *AHEM* SEE YOU AT CAMP ON MONDAY.

OKAY...BYE, SWEETIE. IT WAS NICE TO SEE YOU.
IS SOMETHING WRONG? YOU'RE BOTH ACTING VERY STRANGE.
NOTHING'S **WRONG**, EXCEPT THAT I HAVE BEEN SEEN IN PUBLIC IN THIS HUMILIATING DRESS. CAN WE **PLEASE** GET OUT OF HERE NOW?
ROOM
SLAM!
5 ITEMS
MY KNEES WERE SHAKING WITH RELIEF AND BOTTLED-UP STRESS. IS IT POSSIBLE TO GIVE YOURSELF AN ULCER IN 5 MINUTES? AT THE RIPE AGE OF 12?
YOU KNOW, SOME WOMEN FIND SHOPPING TO BE A RELAXING AND ENJOYABLE EXPERIENCE. IMAGINE THAT.
I DIDN'T BOTHER TO ANSWER. I WAS SO CONFUSED. WHY DID NICOLE SAVE MY HIDE BACK THERE IN YOUNG MISSES?

UNLESS. . . UNLESS SHE PLANNED TO USE THIS INFORMATION AGAINST ME LATER, AND SOMEHOW GET ME INTO EVEN BIGGER TROUBLE.
AND THEN. . . IT HIT ME. LIKE A TON OF BRICKS.
OH, NO.
WHAT? WHAT IS IT?
NOTHING.
THE FLYER. THEY HAD THE FLYER FOR THE ROLLER DERBY BOUT. CLEARLY, NICOLE AND RACHEL WERE PLANNING SOME BIG, ROTTEN REVENGE TO EMBARRASS ME AT THE BOUT. IN FRONT OF 500 PEOPLE.
WELL, IT WAS OBVIOUS WHAT I HAD TO DO. I JUST HAD TO GET THEM BEFORE THEY GOT ME.

CHAPTER • 12

YOU KNOW HOW PICASSO HAD HIS "BLUE PERIOD"?*
*YOU WOULD KNOW THIS IF YOUR MOM FORCED EVENINGS OF CULTURAL ENLIGHTENMENT ON YOU.
WELL, I'VE COME TO CONSIDER THIS PART OF MY LIFE AS MY "BLACK PERIOD."
NIGHTMARES KEPT ME UP ALL NIGHT.
YOU COST US THE GAME, YOU JERK!
WHY WAS I EVER FRIENDS WITH SUCH A LOSER?
SMILE FOR THE YEARBOOK, ASS-TURD!

INSTEAD OF PRACTICING, I SPENT MY FREE TIME DREAMING UP REVENGE ON NICOLE AND RACHEL.
orthwest
Dance
cademy
Summer
Recital
July 30th, 7 pm
Supplies needed:
Rotten eggs
Water balloons
Rotten fruit (various)
Shaving cream?
TOO BAD THEIR RECITAL WAS THE WEEK AFTER MY BOUT. OH WELL. AT LEAST I'D BE PREPARED.

MY DAYS AT CAMP WEREN'T MUCH BETTER.
ZOEY WASN'T TALKING TO ME.
I JUST COULDN'T GET EXCITED ABOUT THE BOUT, NOW THAT I WASN'T JAMMING.
I THINK OUR TEAM NAME SHOULD BE "THE COLD ONES"!
YEAH, WE CAN DRESS UP LIKE VAMPIRES!
YEAH!
WITH ONLY A WEEK TO GO, WE PRACTICED OUR POSITIONS ALL DAY, EVERY DAY. IF IT WAS POSSIBLE, I SEEMED TO BE GETTING EVEN **WORSE** AT BLOCKING. EVERY TIME I TRIED TO HIT SOMEONE, I GOT SENT TO THE PENALTY BOX.
TWEET!
ASTRID! KEEP YOUR ELBOWS IN! PENALTY BOX!
TWEET!
THAT WAS A LOW BLOCK! PENALTY BOX!
REMEMBER, YOU ARE NO HELP AT ALL TO YOUR TEAM WHILE YOU'RE IN THE BOX!

WHEN I **DID** STAY OUT OF THE BOX...
OK, HERE COMES THE JAMMER...
THERE'S THE JAMMER! ON THE INSIDE! HIT HER, ASTRID! HIT HER!
SWING
MISS
GROAN
... I STILL WASN'T MUCH HELP.
ZOEY WASN'T DOING MUCH BETTER AS A JAMMER. SHE HAD A HARD TIME GETTING PAST THE OTHER TEAM'S WALLS.
PANT
PANT
HMMPH.

TIME REALLY FLIES WHEN YOU'RE HAVING... NOT FUN.
MONDAY
TUESDAY
WEDNESDAY
THURSDAY
BEFORE I KNEW IT, THERE WERE ONLY TWO DAYS TO GO UNTIL THE BOUT.
WHEN I **WASN'T** GETTING PUMMELLED BY BRAIDY AND HER TEAM...
... I WAS WATCHING **ZOEY** GET PUMMELLED BY BRAIDY AND HER TEAM.
COLD ONES! BRING IT IN!
THE NEXT JAM IS GOING TO BE THE LAST ONE FOR TODAY.

BLOCKERS, I WANT ASTRID, RUTHLESS, DRACULOLA, AND MINNIE. ZOEY, YOU'RE JAMMER.
SIGH.
ASTRID, I WANT YOU TO HOLD THE INSIDE LINE. DON'T MOVE FROM IT, DON'T LET THE OTHER JAMMER SNEAK PAST YOU.
I'M GOING TO STAY IN MY WALL THIS TIME. CLOSE TO THE LINE. DON'T LET THE JAMMER THROUGH.
HERE'S THE THING ABOUT PLAYING DERBY– THINGS GET REALLY CONFUSING, REALLY FAST.
JAMMER COMING!
HIT HER! HIT HER!
HOLD HER BACK!
WATCH THE INSIDE!
SUDDENLY, I CAUGHT A GLIMPSE OF A STAR! I WAS GOING TO DO IT THIS TIME! I GAVE IT ALL I HAD.

TAKE THAT, RACHEL!!
BAM!
I HIT SOMEONE! I FINALLY HIT SOMEONE!
OWWWW.
TWEET TWEET!
EVERYONE TAKE A KNEE! ZOEY, ARE YOU ALL RIGHT?
ZOEY?!
I'M ON **YOUR TEAM**! YOU'RE SUPPOSED TO HIT THE **OTHER** JAMMER, NOT **ME**!
OK, TAKE IT EASY— SHE DIDN'T MEAN TO...
I KNOW YOU'RE JEALOUS BECAUSE I'M A JAMMER. BUT THAT DOESN'T MEAN YOU HAVE TO TRY AND **HURT** ME!
IT HAPPENS, DON'T WORRY.
YEAH, SHE SHOULDN'T HAVE SAID THAT.
IT WAS AN ACCIDENT! I DIDN'T MEAN TO!

I DIDN'T MEAN TO.
I DECIDED TO WALK BACK TO THE APARTMENT THAT DAY. I WAS IN NO HURRY TO GET HOME.

WHEN YOU WANT TO THINK ABOUT ABSOLUTELY NOTHING AT ALL, THERE IS ONLY ONE THING TO DO.
CLICK
SLAM!
DID YOU GET ANY CHIPS?
MOM?
I RAN INTO NICOLE'S MOM AT THE GROCERY STORE JUST NOW.

MY INSIDES TURNED TO ICE.

SHE SAID NICOLE NEVER JOINED THE DERBY BOOT CAMP. THAT SHE HASN'T BEEN GIVING YOU A RIDE HOME EVERY DAY. DO YOU WANT TO EXPLAIN TO ME **WHAT** IS GOING ON?
MOM, I...

JUST **HOW** HAVE YOU BEEN GETTING HOME FROM CAMP?
I... ROLLER SKATE HOME.

MY MOTHER'S FACE DRAINED FROM RED TO WHITE LIKE IN A CARTOON. A CRAZY PART OF ME WANTED TO LAUGH.

HER VOICE GOT LOW AND DANGEROUS.
YOU'VE BEEN ROLLER SKATING FROM OAKS PARK TO OUR APARTMENT EVERY DAY? YOU HAVE TO CROSS A **HIGHWAY** TO GET HOME.
THERE'S A LIGHT. AND A CROSSWALK.

TO YOUR ROOM. **NOW**. WE ARE GOING TO TALK ABOUT THIS ONCE I CALM DOWN.
PART OF ME—THE PART WITH A DEATH WISH—WANTED TO SAY, "WHAT ABOUT THOSE CHIPS?" LUCKILY, THE PART OF ME THAT WANTED TO LIVE OVERRULED.

I SAT STEAMING ON MY BED. I DIDN'T CARE. I WAS FIGHTING WITH EVERYONE ELSE IN THE WORLD; WHY NOT MY MOTHER TOO?
STUPID NICOLE.
PUNCH!
STUPID MOM!
PUNCH!
PUNCH!
AAAARRRRGHH!!!
STUPID ROLLER DERBY.
RIP
ROLLER DERBY
TAKE THAT!

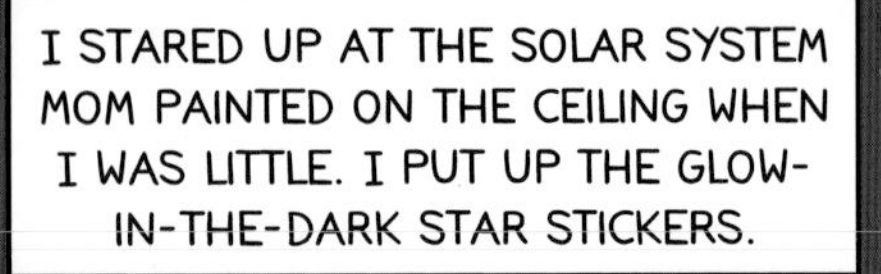
I STARED UP AT THE SOLAR SYSTEM MOM PAINTED ON THE CEILING WHEN I WAS LITTLE. I PUT UP THE GLOW-IN-THE-DARK STAR STICKERS.
I USED TO DO THIS WEIRD THING WHEN I WAS A KID. I USED TO IMAGINE I WAS VENUS, MOM WAS MERCURY, AND NICOLE WAS EARTH.
I'D MAKE UP STORIES ABOUT US FLOATING AROUND THE SOLAR SYSTEM TOGETHER. WE'D VISIT OTHER GALAXIES AND MEET EXTRATERRESTRIALS.
NOW I WAS MORE LIKE A LONE GOLF BALL WHACKED INTO SPACE BY AN ASTRONAUT. JUST FLOATING BY MYSELF. FOREVER.

SOME OF THE LONGEST MOMENTS OF MY LIFE HAVE BEEN SPENT IN MY ROOM, WAITING FOR MOM TO COME IN AND YELL AT ME.

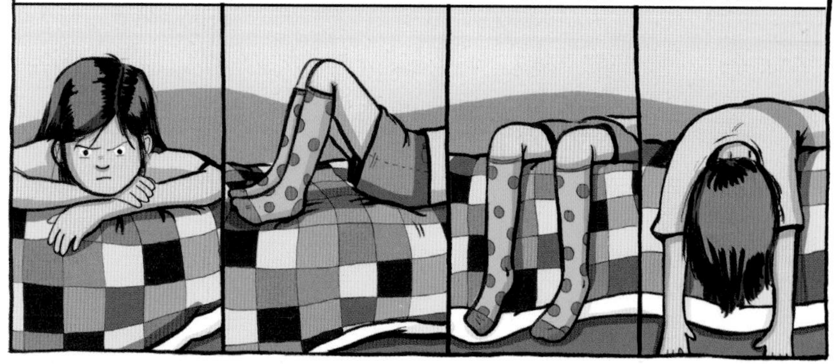

IT WAS WEIRD, THOUGH. SHE JUST SAT THERE. SHE DIDN'T SHOUT. SHE DIDN'T SCREAM. SHE JUST SAT.

I JUST DON'T KNOW WHAT TO DO, ASTRID. FIRST YOU'RE DYEING YOUR HAIR, NOW YOU'RE LYING TO ME...BEING A PARENT WAS SO MUCH EASIER WHEN YOU WERE A LITTLE GIRL.

AND YOU'RE GOING TO BE A TEENAGER SOON. HOW DO I KNOW YOU WON'T LIE TO ME ABOUT SMOKING, OR SKIPPING SCHOOL, OR DOING DRUGS...
WHY DOES EVERYONE THINK I'M DOING DRUGS?
I JUST...I FEEL LIKE I DON'T KNOW WHO YOU ARE ANYMORE.
WELL...MAYBE I DON'T KNOW WHO I AM EITHER!
I DON'T KNOW WHERE **THAT** ONE CAME FROM. FINALLY, MOM LOOKED AT ME.
WHY DID YOU LIE TO ME? WHY DIDN'T YOU TELL ME NICOLE DIDN'T SIGN UP FOR DERBY CAMP?
I DON'T KNOW.
ASTRID, THAT IS NOT **GOOD** ENOUGH. WHY DIDN'T YOU TELL ME?
I DIDN'T TELL YOU, BECAUSE...BECAUSE I KNEW WHAT YOU WOULD SAY. YOU'D SAY, "OH, YOU AND NICOLE ARE JUST HAVING A FIGHT, YOU'LL MAKE UP SOON." BUT IT'S **NOT** THAT, IT'S **SOMETHING** ELSE, BUT I **DON'T KNOW WHAT IT IS**.

I WAS KIND OF YELLING BY NOW. ACCORDING TO THE RULES OF FIGHTING, THIS IS WHERE MOM SHOULD HAVE STARTED YELLING TOO. BUT SHE SURPRISED ME BY SAYING QUIETLY:
TELL ME ABOUT IT.
WELL. THAT DID IT.
EVERYTHING IS JUST... ALL SCREWED UP.
IT ALL CAME TUMBLING OUT. HOW NICOLE IS BEST FRIENDS WITH RACHEL NOW. HOW SHE ONLY WANTS TO BE POPULAR, AND ONLY CARES ABOUT CLOTHES, AND MAKEUP, AND BOYS.
I TOLD HER HOW SHE PLANNED TO DITCH ME IN JUNIOR HIGH, AND ABOUT THE SODA, AND ABOUT HOW THEY WERE GOING TO MAKE LIFE MISERABLE FOR ME NEXT YEAR.
SINCE I WAS ON A ROLL, I ALSO TOLD HER ABOUT ZOEY, AND HOW I HAD LOST HER AS A FRIEND TOO. HOW I WASN'T A JAMMER IN THE BOUT, AND HOW I WAS GOING TO MAKE A FOOL OF MYSELF IN FRONT OF 500 PEOPLE ON SATURDAY.

YOU'VE HAD ALL OF THIS BOTTLED UP INSIDE OF YOU FOR WEEKS? SWEETIE, IF YOU KEEP ALL YOUR FEELINGS INSIDE LIKE THIS, YOU'RE GOING TO EXPLODE.
I WAS EMPTY NOW, AND I FELT SO, SO TIRED.
MOM? CAN YOU JUST HUG ME FOR A LITTLE BIT?
OF COURSE, SWEETIE.
YOU'RE GOING THROUGH A DIFFICULT TIME RIGHT NOW. BEING A TEENAGER CAN BE REALLY CONFUSING.
OH NO. NOT **THIS** TALK AGAIN!
...AND I NEVER DID LIKE RACHEL. OR HER MOM.
REALLY?
THAT MADE ME FEEL BETTER.
HEY MOM?
I KNEW THIS WASN'T THE BEST TIME TO ASK. BUT I HAD TO KNOW.

TOUGHER.
STRONGER.
FEARLESS.
AM I STILL ALLOWED TO PLAY IN THE BOUT?
IN THAT SPLIT SECOND, I KNEW. EVEN THOUGH I STUNK, AND I WASN'T A JAMMER, AND I MIGHT EMBARRASS MYSELF IN FRONT OF A HUGE CROWD...I STILL WANTED TO PLAY.
PLEASE.
DO YOU **PROMISE** TO BE HONEST WITH ME FROM NOW ON? I THINK THE ONLY WAY WE'RE GOING TO GET THROUGH THESE NEXT FEW YEARS IS IF I'M HONEST WITH YOU, AND YOU'RE HONEST WITH ME. DEAL?
DEAL.
AND EVEN THOUGH NOTHING HAD REALLY CHANGED— I STILL HAD 2 ENEMIES PLOTTING TO GET ME, AND I STILL HAD NO IDEA HOW I'D SURVIVE THE BOUT— I FELT A LOT BETTER.
AND— WAIT A SECOND— DID I JUST GET OUT OF BEING IN TROUBLE?!
I'M A GENIUS!
SO TAKE IT FROM ME, KIDS: IF YOU FIND YOURSELF IN HOT WATER WITH YOUR PARENTS,
TRY TALKING TO THEM ABOUT YOUR "CRAZY, MIXED-UP TEENAGE FEELINGS." IT MIGHT JUST GET YOU OUT OF A JAM.
WINK

CHAPTER 13
I SPOKE TOO SOON— I WASN'T COMPLETELY OUT OF HOT WATER YET.
YOU KNOW WHAT WE HAVE TO DO NOW, RIGHT?
HAVE SOME ICE-CREAM SUNDAES? THAT'S FUNNY, THAT'S JUST WHAT I WAS THINKING! WE REALLY ARE A GOOD TEAM.
VERY FUNNY. GET YOUR SHOES ON.
SIGH
ROLLER DE
TOUGHER. STRONGER. FEARLESS. TOUGHER. STRONGER. FEARLESS. TOUGHER. STRONGER. FEARLESS.
TOUGHER. STRONGER. FEARLESS. TOUGHER. STRONGER. FEARLESS. TOUGHER. STRONGER. FEARLESS.

DING DONG
WELL, YOUR HAIR REALLY IS BLUE, ISN'T IT.
HI, JOANNE. SORRY TO BOTHER YOU, BUT ASTRID HAS SOMETHING SHE'D LIKE TO SAY TO YOU.
I'M SORRY I LIED ABOUT YOU DRIVING ME HOME. NICOLE DIDN'T KNOW ANYTHING ABOUT IT, SO SHE SHOULDN'T GET IN TROUBLE. IT'S MY FAULT.
WELL, THANK YOU FOR TELLING ME THAT, ASTRID. I'M JUST GLAD YOU DIDN'T GET HURT, AND I HOPE YOU'VE LEARNED YOUR LESSON.
I GUESS THAT MEANS YOU'RE OFF YOUR GROUNDING, NICOLE.
SLAM!
DO YOU HAVE SOMETHING TO SAY TO NICOLE, TOO?
CAN I DO IT IN PRIVATE? PLEASE?
ALL RIGHT. GO ON UP.

I TOOK MY SHOES OFF BEFORE I WENT UPSTAIRS. NO SENSE IN GETTING ON MRS. B.'S BAD SIDE A MINUTE AFTER APOLOGIZING.
Nicole
TOUGHER. STRONGER. FEARLESS.
KNOCK KNOCK
CAN I COME IN?
ALL RIGHT.

PARIS
WELL? ARE YOU HERE TO THROW SOMETHING ELSE AT ME?
IT POPPED OUT OF MY MOUTH BEFORE I COULD THINK ABOUT IT.
WHY DIDN'T YOU TELL ON ME THAT DAY AT THE MALL?
I THOUGHT YOU WERE SUPPOSED TO BE **APOLOGIZING** TO ME.
I KNOW, BUT... I JUST WANT TO KNOW.
IT'S JUST...IT SEEMS WEIRD, ALL THIS FIGHTING. YOU'VE BEEN MY BEST FRIEND FOR SO LONG...I COULDN'T JUST TELL ON YOU. EVEN AFTER...AFTER EVERYTHING.
THIS WAS THE HARDEST QUESTION TO ASK.
WHY DID YOU DITCH ME FOR RACHEL?

I DIDN'T DITCH YOU. WE'RE GOING TO JUNIOR HIGH– WE SHOULD MAKE SOME NEW FRIENDS. THERE'S NOTHING WRONG WITH MAKING NEW FRIENDS.
YEAH, BUT RACHEL?
IT'S JUST... SHE LIKES THE SAME THINGS I DO. LIKE BALLET, AND DANCE.
AND I CAN TALK TO HER ABOUT BOYS...
YECH.
...AND SHE DOESN'T ACT ALL WEIRD ABOUT IT.
HMMPH.
NOW NICOLE WAS ON HER OWN ROLL.
WE ALWAYS DID WHAT YOU WANTED TO DO. LIKE ROLLER SKATING, OR THE SCIENCE MUSEUM. YOU NEVER WANTED TO DO THE THINGS I LIKE.
OH.
I GUESS IT'S BECAUSE THE THINGS I LIKE ARE "SHALLOW" AND "BORING." RIGHT?
I DIDN'T MEAN THAT.
YEAH. RIGHT.

IT'S JUST... YOU ACT SO DIFFERENT WHEN YOU'RE AROUND RACHEL.
YOU'RE DIFFERENT NOW TOO.
IN CASE YOU HAVEN'T NOTICED.
WHAT HAPPENED TO YOUR FEET?
IT'S FROM POINTE. MY TOES GET ALL BLOODY, AND I HAVE TO TAPE THEM.
HEY, ME TOO! I GET THESE BIG BLISTERS FROM MY SKATES.

ARE THOSE YOUR POINTE SHOES?
YEAH.
DOES IT HURT A LOT? DOING POINTE?
WELL, YEAH. BUT YOU JUST HAVE TO SUCK IT UP.
I NEVER KNEW BALLET WAS SO HARD-CORE.
YOU NEVER ASKED.
ASTRID? IT'S TIME TO GET GOING. WE SHOULD LET THEM HAVE THEIR DINNER.
OH. WELL. SEE YA.
OK. UM, BYE.
YORK CITY Ballet
OH, AND SORRY ABOUT THE WHOLE LYING ABOUT DERBY CAMP THING.

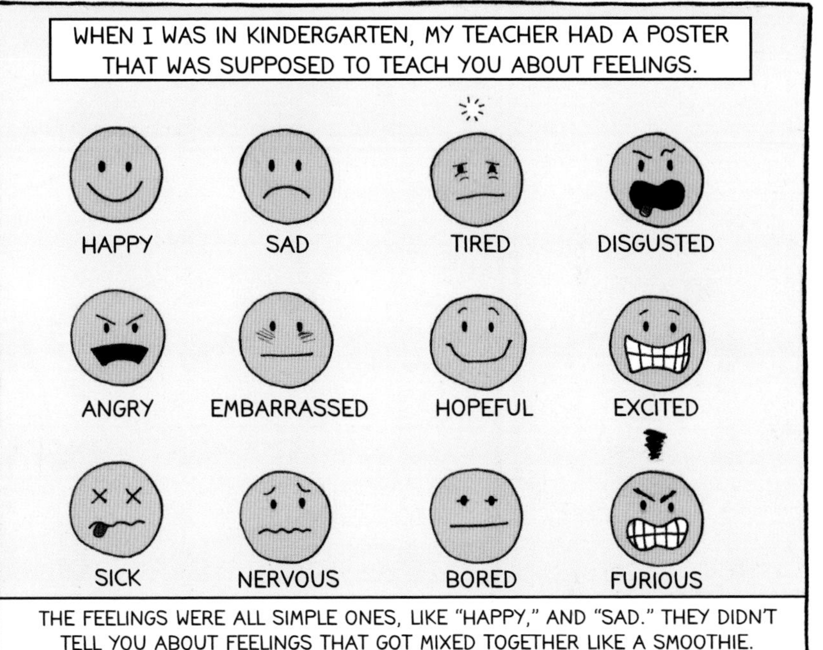
WHEN I WAS IN KINDERGARTEN, MY TEACHER HAD A POSTER THAT WAS SUPPOSED TO TEACH YOU ABOUT FEELINGS.
HAPPY
SAD
TIRED
DISGUSTED
ANGRY
EMBARRASSED
HOPEFUL
EXCITED
SICK
NERVOUS
BORED
FURIOUS
THE FEELINGS WERE ALL SIMPLE ONES, LIKE "HAPPY," AND "SAD." THEY DIDN'T TELL YOU ABOUT FEELINGS THAT GOT MIXED TOGETHER LIKE A SMOOTHIE.

I FELT BETTER... BUT NOT COMPLETELY. I WAS STILL A LITTLE MAD AT NICOLE... BUT I FELT LIKE I DID SOMETHING WRONG TOO. I WAS HAPPY THAT I TALKED TO HER... BUT SAD THAT EVERYTHING STILL FELT SO DIFFERENT.

I WAS SHAD.
?
HAPPY
+
SAD
=
SHAD

CHAPTER 14
I WOKE UP THE NEXT MORNING FEELING
NERVOUS
+
SICK
=
NERSICK
OUR LAST PRACTICE BEFORE THE BOUT. I PUT ON MY DEMENTED LEPRECHAUN SHIRT— I NEEDED ALL THE LUCK I COULD GET.
I GUESS IT WORKED, BECAUSE...
WHEN I GOT TO THE HANGAR, I SAW A NOTE. I HADN'T LEFT HER ONE IN WEEKS.
Dear Dud,
Congratulations! I hear all the new Rosebuds will be playing tomorrow night. Tell me your name, and I'll make a poster to cheer you on!
-Bitey
P.S.— You're probably scared, and nervous, and just about ready to pee your pants. But don't run from your fear. Embrace it! Because believe me...
...the best things in life are worth fighting for.

ZOEY, I'M... I'M SORRY.
I'VE BEEN A REAL JERK. AND I DIDN'T MEAN TO HIT YOU YESTERDAY. I'M JUST A TERRIBLE BLOCKER. OK? THAT'S THE TRUTH.
I DON'T KNOW WHAT I EXPECTED TO HAPPEN...
FRIENDS FOREVER!!
OH ASTRID, I FORGIVE YOU. YOU SHOULD TAKE MY PLACE AS JAMMER TOMORROW. LET'S BE FRIENDS, FOREVER AND EVER AND EVER!
BUT HERE IS WHAT ACTUALLY HAPPENED:
OK.
OK? SO... YOU FORGIVE ME?
SURE. WHATEVER.
TWEET TWEET!

LADIES, THIS IS OUR LAST PRACTICE BEFORE THE BOUT TOMORROW NIGHT! WE'RE GOING TO SCRIMMAGE FOR A BIT— AND THEN WE'RE GOING TO HAVE A LITTLE PARTY!
YAY!
WOO HOO!
YOUR T-SHIRTS FOR THE BOUT CAME IN, AND WE BROUGHT SOME PUFFY PAINT AND MARKERS SO YOU CAN DECORATE YOUR UNIFORMS.
SO! GET WITH YOUR TEAMS, AND LET'S GET GOING!
AFTER WEEKS OF TOUGH TRAINING...
AND EXTRA PRACTICES...
...WITH LOTS OF BLOOD, SWEAT, AND TEARS...
...I CAN SAY, WITHOUT A DOUBT...
...I STILL STUNK.
MISS
GROAN
HEH HEH.
FOR ONCE, I WAS GLAD TO BE A BLOCKER. AT LEAST I'D BLEND INTO THE CROWD. MAYBE NO ONE WOULD NOTICE WHEN I SCREWED UP.

IT'S NOT LIKE BEING A JAMMER.
ALL THE BLOCKERS OUT FOR YOUR BLOOD...
SLAM!
ALL ALONE ON THE TRACK... HUNDREDS OF EYES IN THE AUDIENCE ON YOU...
...AND ONLY YOU.
SUDDENLY, I RECOGNIZED THE LOOK ON ZOEY'S FACE.
TERROR
SICK
TERROR ZOMBIE
TWEET TWEET!
OK, THAT'S IT! LET'S EAT PIZZA AND HAVE SOME FUN!
ZOEY? YOU'RE GOING TO BE GREAT TOMORROW NIGHT, YOU KNOW.
UH-HUH.
REALLY. YOU'LL BE GREAT. YOU... YOU DESERVE TO BE A JAMMER.
HAVE YOU **SEEN** ME JAM RECENTLY? I'M TERRIBLE. I DON'T KNOW WHY THEY PICKED ME IN THE FIRST PLACE.

ZOEY...
JUST FORGET IT.
I TRIED HAVING FUN AT THE PARTY... BUT IT WAS HARD, WITH ZOEY LOOKING SO MISERABLE.
WE GOT OUR TEAM T-SHIRTS.
COOL!
ASTRID, WHAT'S YOUR DERBY NAME GOING TO BE?
OH! ...I HAVE NO IDEA!
WITH EVERYTHING GOING ON... I HAD COMPLETELY FORGOTTEN I NEEDED A DERBY NAME FOR TOMORROW NIGHT!
WHAT ABOUT PHOENIX?
KRAKEN SKULLS!
BUMBLE-BEE?
THOSE WERE ALL GOOD... BUT NOT EXACTLY RIGHT. I'D HAVE TO COME UP WITH MY OWN.

OK, LADIES, TIME TO GO! BE HERE TOMORROW NIGHT AT 5 PM. THE ADULT BOUT STARTS AT 6 PM. YOU'LL BE SKATING AT HALFTIME, AROUND 6:45 OR SO.
REMEMBER TO EAT PLENTY OF PROTEIN, AND DRINK LOTS OF WATER THROUGHOUT THE DAY.
AND NO MATTER WHAT HAPPENS, WIN OR LOSE... JUST TRY TO ENJOY THE JOURNEY.
MAKE SURE YOU SEE NAPOLEON ON YOUR WAY OUT— EACH OF YOU GETS 3 FREE TICKETS TO THE BOUT FOR YOUR FAMILY AND FRIENDS.
PIZZA
PIZZA
ZOEY! I JUST WANTED TO SAY...
BUT THERE WAS NOTHING ELSE TO SAY. BUT MAYBE THERE WAS SOMETHING I COULD **DO**.
BEEP BEEP!
ASTRID! COME ON! I HAVE TO BE BACK AT WORK IN 20 MINUTES!
I FORGOT ONE THING, MOM! I'LL BE OUT IN TWO SECONDS.
ASTRID! HURRY UP!

Dear Rainbow,

Thank you for all of your notes. I will keep them all forever.

As for the sign, I think I'd rather stay anonymous for now.

But if you'd like to make a sign for Slay Miserables, I think she can use all the help she can get.

Sincerely,

Rose Dud

IT WASN'T MUCH... BUT MAYBE IT WOULD HELP.

EXIT

ROSE CITY ROLLERS

TRASH

BESIDES, I DIDN'T WANT RAINBOW TO KNOW HOW TERRIBLE I WAS, ANYWAY.

REMEMBER HOW I SAID I WASN'T COMPLETELY OUT OF HOT WATER YET?
MOM SAID I COULDN'T STAY HOME BY MYSELF ANYMORE. I'D HAVE TO SPEND MY AFTERNOONS AT WORK WITH HER. FOR THE **REST OF THE SUMMER**.

MOM WORKS AS A LIBRARIAN AT THE LOCAL UNIVERSITY.
SHE LIKES IT, BUT THE REAL REASON SHE WORKS THERE IS SO I CAN GO TO COLLEGE THERE FOR FREE, AND THAT I'D BETTER REMEMBER THAT WHEN SHE'S OLD AND GRAY AND I WANT TO PUT HER IN A NURSING HOME.
A LIBRARY IS NOT A HOTBED OF ACTION ON A GOOD DAY... BUT DURING THE SUMMER, WITH BARELY ANYONE THERE...
SIGH.
STAY IN THIS AREA, OK? I GET OFF TODAY AT 4. I'LL COME AND CHECK ON YOU DURING MY BREAK.

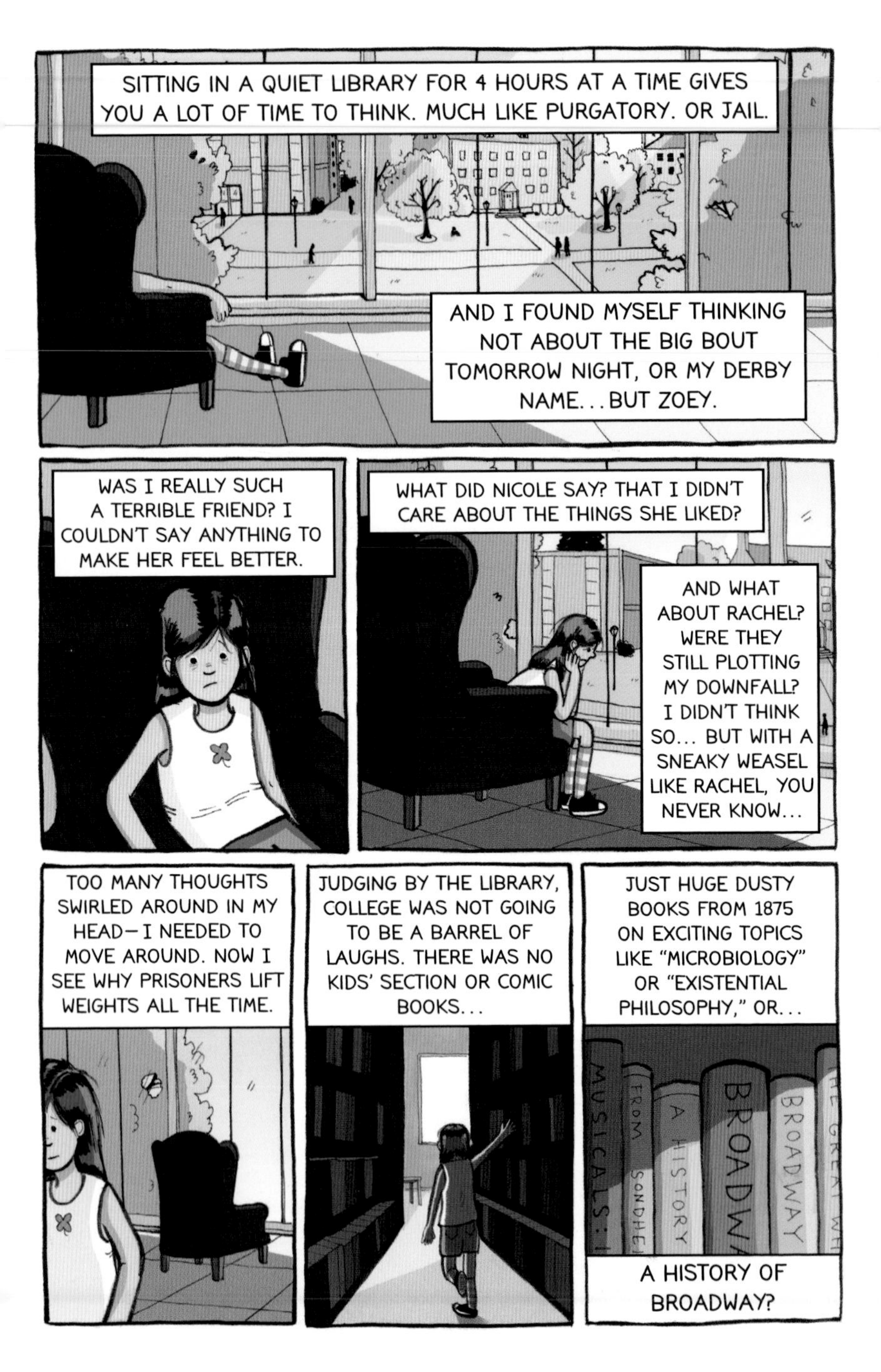
SITTING IN A QUIET LIBRARY FOR 4 HOURS AT A TIME GIVES YOU A LOT OF TIME TO THINK. MUCH LIKE PURGATORY. OR JAIL.
AND I FOUND MYSELF THINKING NOT ABOUT THE BIG BOUT TOMORROW NIGHT, OR MY DERBY NAME... BUT ZOEY.
WAS I REALLY SUCH A TERRIBLE FRIEND? I COULDN'T SAY ANYTHING TO MAKE HER FEEL BETTER.
WHAT DID NICOLE SAY? THAT I DIDN'T CARE ABOUT THE THINGS SHE LIKED?
AND WHAT ABOUT RACHEL? WERE THEY STILL PLOTTING MY DOWNFALL? I DIDN'T THINK SO... BUT WITH A SNEAKY WEASEL LIKE RACHEL, YOU NEVER KNOW...
TOO MANY THOUGHTS SWIRLED AROUND IN MY HEAD—I NEEDED TO MOVE AROUND. NOW I SEE WHY PRISONERS LIFT WEIGHTS ALL THE TIME.
JUDGING BY THE LIBRARY, COLLEGE WAS NOT GOING TO BE A BARREL OF LAUGHS. THERE WAS NO KIDS' SECTION OR COMIC BOOKS...
JUST HUGE DUSTY BOOKS FROM 1875 ON EXCITING TOPICS LIKE "MICROBIOLOGY" OR "EXISTENTIAL PHILOSOPHY," OR...
MUSICALS:
FROM SONDHE
A HISTORY
BROADWA
BROADWAY
A HISTORY OF BROADWAY?

BROADWAY
42nd STREET
A BOOK WITH FULL-PAGE HUGH JACKMAN PHOTOS? ZOEY WOULD **LOVE** THIS.
I SUDDENLY HAD AN IDEA. A GOOD ONE.
MOM? COULD I PLEASE BORROW SOME GLUE? AND SCISSORS, AND A MARKER?
DON'T BE RUDE— SAY HELLO TO MRS. KEMP.
ASTRID! YOU'RE GETTING SO BIG!
...IS THAT THE SHIRT...
HERE YOU GO, HONEY. RUN ON UPSTAIRS— I'LL CHECK ON YOU IN A BIT.
SHOVE
TOP O' THE MORNING TO YOU, MRS. KEMP!
I STILL HAD $4.75 LEFT OVER FROM MY WEEKLY EMERGENCY FUND— MOM FORGOT TO TAKE THAT BACK FROM ME. PHOTOCOPIES WERE $.02, SO THAT MEANT I COULD MAKE EXACTLY...
COPIES $.02

... A LOT OF COPIES.
I KNEW WE HAD A BUNCH OF POPSICLE STICKS IN THE CRAFT BUCKET AT HOME. IT LOOKED LIKE I HAD A LONG NIGHT OF WORK AHEAD OF ME.
READY TO GO?
WHAT ON EARTH ARE YOU DOING?
CAN WE MAKE A STOP ON THE WAY HOME? IT'S REALLY IMPORTANT.

ONE THING ABOUT SKATING AROUND TOWN... I WAS PRETTY GOOD AT DIRECTIONS NOW.
MAKE A LEFT, AND... IT'S AT THE END OF THIS STREET.
REEDWAY
I'LL BE RIGHT BACK.
SHUT UP, ZOEY!
STOP SITTING ON ME!
DING DONG
I'LL GET IT!
YOUR FACE WILL SCARE VISITORS AWAY—**I'LL** GET IT!
OK, FLOOR IT, MOM!
ZOEY? SOMEONE LEFT A WEIRD VOODOO DOLL FOR YOU.
Hugh Jackman says: You'll do great tomorrow.
MOM? IS IT OK IF WE MAKE **ONE FINAL** STOP?

IN A FEW SHORT MINUTES, WE WERE THERE.
I'M PROUD OF YOU, HONEY. ARE YOU SURE YOU DON'T WANT ME TO COME WITH YOU?
I'M SURE. I HAVE TO DO THIS MYSELF.
IN FACT, I WASN'T SURE I SHOULD DO THIS AT ALL. BUT I KEPT THINKING ABOUT RAINBOW BITE'S NOTE. I COULD KEEP RUNNING FROM MY BATTLES AND LIVE IN FEAR...
... OR I COULD EMBRACE THE FEAR.
NICOLE! RACHEL!
WHAT ARE **YOU** DOING HERE? I THOUGHT I TOLD YOU TO STAY AWAY FROM US. DO I NEED TO GET A RESTRAINING ORDER AGAINST YOU?
LOOK, I HAVE TWO EXTRA TICKETS TO MY ROLLER DERBY BOUT TOMORROW NIGHT. AND... I WANT YOU TO HAVE THEM. I WANT A TRUCE.

A **TRUCE**? ARE YOU SERIOUS? AFTER WHAT YOU DID TO US? AND WHY WOULD WE WANT TO COME TO YOUR STUPID–
AND THEN, I HEARD IT. THE MOST BEAUTIFUL SOUND IN THE WORLD... NICOLE INTERRUPTED RACHEL.
THANKS, ASTRID. THAT'S... REALLY NICE OF YOU.
SURE. AND... I'M GOING TO COME TO YOUR BALLET RECITAL NEXT WEEK. NOT LIKE YOU HAVE TO COME TOMORROW OR ANYTHING. I JUST... I WANTED YOU TO KNOW.
UM, SO– SEE YOU.
YEAH, SEE YOU.
MAYBE THIS WAS A STUPID IDEA. MAYBE I SHOULD HAVE HANDED THEM SOME ROTTEN EGGS AND TOMATOES TO THROW AT ME WHILE I WAS AT IT. BUT NOW, NO MATTER WHAT HAPPENED TOMORROW...
...I STILL FELT LIKE I WON SOMETHING TODAY.
SCORE:
ME: 1
RACHEL: 0

CHAPTER 15
WHEN I WOKE UP THE NEXT MORNING, I DIDN'T HOP OUT OF BED RIGHT AWAY. A SWARM OF BUTTERFLIES ATTACKED MY STOMACH. THIS WAS IT. IT WAS FINALLY HERE. BOUT DAY.
I'D STAYED UP UNTIL MIDNIGHT LAST NIGHT WORKING ON MY SECRET PROJECT. I STILL HADN'T THOUGHT OF A DERBY NAME.
I STARED UP AT THE CEILING, AS IF I'D FIND MY ANSWER IN THE PAINTED UNIVERSE.
SO MUCH HAD CHANGED OVER THE SUMMER. I DIDN'T FEEL LIKE ONE OF THOSE PLANETS ANYMORE, MOVING IN ORBIT WITH NICOLE AND MOM BY MY SIDE.
BUT MAYBE I WASN'T A LONE GOLF BALL, EITHER.

I HAD NO IDEA WHAT WAS GOING TO HAPPEN TONIGHT. MAYBE I'D DO A GOOD JOB...
ON TOP OF THE WORLD, HA-HA
OR MAYBE I'D MAKE A TOTAL FOOL OUT OF MYSELF.
BLACK HOLE OF DESPAIR
WHAT DID HEIDI SAY? ENJOY THE JOURNEY? EASY FOR **HER** TO SAY— WHAT IF THIS JOURNEY ENDED IN THE FIERY FLAMES OF DESTRUCTION?
AND JUST LIKE THAT, IT CAME TO ME. MY ROLLER DERBY NAME.

ONLY A FEW HOURS BEFORE I HAD TO BE AT THE HANGAR, AND I HAD A LOT TO DO.
I HAD TO PUT MY NAME AND NUMBER ON THE BACK OF MY SHIRT.
I HAD TO DECORATE MY HELMET...WHICH REQUIRED A LITTLE CREATIVE THINKING.
WHAT ARE YOU DOING IN THERE, ASTRID?
NOTHING! DON'T COME IN!
I HAD TO PUT MY UNIFORM TOGETHER.
OLD GYM SHORTS
UNIFORM SHIRT
BANDANA TAKEN FROM BEAR
BLUE TIGHTS FROM LAST YEAR'S HALLOWEEN COSTUME
(SUPERMAN, IF YOU WANT TO KNOW.)

THEN, I UTTERED WORDS I NEVER THOUGHT I'D SAY...
MOM?
CAN YOU HELP ME WITH MY MAKEUP?
MOM WAS THERE IN 1.7 SECONDS.
OH! OUR FIRST MOTHER-DAUGHTER MAKEUP SESSION!
WHEN YOU'RE PUTTING ON EYELINER, YOU WANT TO STAY AS CLOSE TO YOUR EYELASHES AS YOU CAN.
OPEN YOUR EYES **REALLY** WIDE WHEN YOU'RE PUTTING ON MASCARA.
THE KEY IS TO LOOK NATURAL.
NATURAL. GOT IT. NOW...CAN YOU SHOW ME HOW TO LOOK LIKE A BLOOD-SUCKING VAMPIRE?
SIGH

FINALLY...
I WAS READY.
ROLLER DERBY
THIS WAS ME.
ASTEROID
BURNING A FIERY PATH THROUGH TIME AND SPACE.

ASTRID! TIME TO GET A MOVE ON!
NO, SOMETHING WAS MISSING...
JUST A SECOND, MOM!
12
Asteroid
THERE.

WHEN WE GOT TO THE HANGAR, I STARTED TO GET REALLY, REALLY NERVOUS. I'D NEVER SEEN IT SO CROWDED BEFORE.
I SAW VOLUNTEERS, ANNOUNCERS, ADULT SKATERS...
6
OLUNTE
... BUT NO ZOEY.
WE'RE MEETING OUTSIDE IN 15 MINUTES! SPREAD THE WORD.
HEY! AND NICE NAME... ASTEROID.
15 MINUTES. THAT SHOULD BE JUST ENOUGH TIME TO ACTIVATE MY SECRET PLAN.
I HAD TO DO IT NOW, BEFORE SOMEONE NOTICED AND ASKED WHAT I WAS DOING.

HI! COULD YOU PASS THESE AROUND? THEY'RE FOR THE HALFTIME BOUT.
HI! FOR THE HALFTIME BOUT!
PASS THEM AROUND! HALFTIME BOUT PROPS!
I STILL DIDN'T SEE ZOEY... **OR** NICOLE.
I COULD SEE MOM, THOUGH. A LITTLE **TOO** WELL.
ASTRID! ASTRID HONEY! OVER HERE!
I HANDED OUT THE REST OF MY PROPS, AND HEADED TOWARD THE BATHROOM FOR ABOUT THE 100TH TIME TODAY.
RESTROOMS
WHAT THE HECK **ARE** THESE THINGS?
AND WHO SHOULD I FIND IN THERE BUT...
ZOEY?

I CAN'T DO THIS. I'M NOT READY. HAVE YOU SEEN HOW MANY PEOPLE ARE OUT THERE?
YOU **ARE** READY FOR THIS! REMEMBER HOW YOU STAYED AFTER PRACTICE FOR TWO WHOLE WEEKS? YOU'VE **GOT** THIS!
SHE DIDN'T LOOK CONVINCED.
OK, WELL... THINK OF THIS AS A PERFORMANCE PIECE! EVEN IF YOU FAIL MISERABLY... YOU CAN STILL USE THAT IN YOUR ACTING, RIGHT?
THIS HAD TO QUALIFY AS THE WORST PEP TALK OF ALL TIME. BUT TO MY SURPRISE...
THAT... THAT'S TRUE, ACTUALLY. THE SHOW MUST GO ON, RIGHT?
BESIDES, HUGH JACKMAN BELIEVES IN ME.
I WAITED WHILE ZOEY WASHED HER FACE. I HANDED HER A PILE OF PAPER TOWELS WHEN SHE WAS DONE.
246
Slay Miserables
YOU READY?
246
Slay Miserables
12
Asteroi

246
Slay Miserables
12
Asteroid
LET'S DO THIS.

CHAPTER 16
THE COACHES DECIDED WE SHOULD SKATE AROUND THE PARKING LOT WHILE WE WAITED FOR HALFTIME. THAT WAY WE'D BE WARMED UP WHEN IT WAS TIME TO GO.
PLUS, THEY FIGURED WE'D BE LESS NERVOUS IF WE STAYED AWAY FROM THE CROWDS.
ROAR!
CHEER!
BEFORE I KNEW IT...
OK, YOU'VE GOT ABOUT FIVE MINUTES UNTIL YOU'RE ON!
LET'S HAVE TEAM COLD ONES HERE.
TEAM BLACK DEATH OVER HERE.
WHEN I CALL YOUR TEAM NAME, SKATE ONE LAP TOGETHER, WAVE TO THE AUDIENCE— AND THEN GO TO YOUR RESPECTIVE BENCHES.

OH MAN. IT'S HAPPENING. IT'S REALLY HAPPENING. IT'S...
HOW IS IT POSSIBLE FOR BRAIDY PUNCH TO LOOK **EVEN SCARIER** THAN SHE DOES IN REAL LIFE?!
AND, WITH A SCORE OF 79 TO 43, ROSE CITY HEADS INTO THE SECOND HALF WITH THE LEAD! BUT DON'T GO ANYWHERE, FOLKS! GRAB A REFRESHMENT AND SIT RIGHT BACK DOWN, BECAUSE WE HAVE **MORE** DERBY ACTION COMING AT YOU RIGHT NOW!
COMING UP NEXT, THE NEW GENERATION OF ROSE CITY ROLLERS... **THE ROSEBUDS**! THESE SKATERS ARE BETWEEN THE AGES OF 12 AND 17, AND THEY ARE READY TO RUMBLE!
LADIES AND GENTLEMEN, THE FIRST TEAM FOR OUR SPECIAL HALFTIME BOUT, **THE BLACK DEATH!**
AND THEIR OPPONENTS, WEARING ICY BLUE...
12
Asteroid
2462
Slay Miserables
HERE WE GO...

THE COLD ONES!

Whoo!

THE FLASHES OF THE CAMERAS LOOKED LIKE STARS. IT WAS HANDS DOWN ONE OF THE BEST MOMENTS OF MY LIFE. . .

Clap!

Yeah!

Yeah!

Cheer!

... SO FAR.

IS THAT...
ARE THOSE...
... A WHOLE BUNCH OF HUGH JACKMAN MASKS?
GO SLAY!
GO SLAY
GO SLAY MISERABLES!
GO SLAY MISERABLES!
IS THAT **RAINBOW BITE**? HOLDING A SIGN? FOR **ME**?

COLD ONES!
BRING IT IN!
LET'S DO OUR
CHEER!
1-2-3. . .
COLD ONES!
NOW SHOW
ME YOUR
WARFACE!
AAAAAAAAAGGHHHHHHHH!!!!!
NOW GET OUT
THERE AND
DO ME PROUD!
ZOEY! I MEAN, SLAY! YOU'RE JAMMING
FIRST. ASTEROID, YOU'RE BLOCKER #3.
GET OUT THERE, BOTH OF YOU!
246
12

MY FIRST JAM IN AN ACTUAL BOUT! MY FIRST JAM IN...
THUNK
MAYBE YOU'RE WONDERING...HOW DOES IT FEEL TO FALL ON YOUR BUTT IN FRONT OF 500 PEOPLE?
ANSWER: SURPRISINGLY... NOT THAT BAD!
GOT **THAT** OUT OF THE WAY!
AND WE HAVE OUR FIRST LINEUP! ON THE JAMMER LINE WE HAVE SLAY MISERABLES FROM THE COLD ONES. THRILLA GODZILLA IS JAMMING FOR BLACK DEATH!

Go Slay!
Get 'em, Slay!
You got this, Thrilla!
Go Thrilla!
GO, ASTEROID!
GO ASTEROID
SKATERS, READY!
TWEET!
ONCE WE GOT GOING. . . THE CROWD DISAPPEARED AND IT WAS JUST LIKE PRACTICE!
AND I DO MEAN **JUST** LIKE PRACTICE.
SWING
MISS
RATS!

I MANAGED TO DO A FEW THINGS RIGHT, THOUGH!
I HELD THE INSIDE LINE...
...I HAD A NICE BOOTY BLOCK ON THEIR JAMMER ONCE...
...AND I SUCCESSFULLY AVOIDED GETTING HIT BY BRAIDY PUNCH.
GULP
ZOEY WAS DOING PRETTY WELL TOO!
...MOST OF THE TIME.
100
MINNIE ME
3.14
Marz
Black Death
Cold Ones
85
81
Time Remaining:
0:45
THE SCORE WAS REALLY CLOSE THE ENTIRE TIME! AND TO MY SURPRISE... I WAS HAVING **FUN**!
WOO!
YEAH!
SO MUCH FUN, THAT BEFORE I KNEW IT...

A TIME-OUT IS CALLED BY THE COLD ONES! THE SCORE IS BLACK DEATH, 85, COLD ONES, 81. WITH LESS THAN A MINUTE LEFT TO PLAY...
...THIS WILL LIKELY BE THE LAST JAM OF THE GAME!
LADIES, THIS IS IT. **LAST JAM**. WE ARE ONLY FOUR POINTS BEHIND— WE CAN **WIN** THIS.
BLOCKERS, I WANT DRACULOLA, RUTHLESS, PANDA-MONIUM, AND ASTEROID. SLAY, YOU'RE JAMMING.
GULP
ALL OF YOU, KEEP YOUR HEADS AND WE CAN DO THIS. JUST LIKE WE DID IN PRACTICE, OK?
1-2-3...
COLD ONES!
RUTHLESS

I LINED UP ON THE TRACK FOR THE LAST TIME, AND FOUND MYSELF...
... RIGHT NEXT TO BRAIDY PUNCH.
THIS IS OUR GAME, PIPSQUEAK, AND YOU ARE NOT TAKING IT FROM US!
LOOKS LIKE SLAY MISERABLES AND THRILLA GODZILLA ARE OUR LAST JAMMERS OF THE GAME!
TWEET!
OOH, AND THRILLA HITS SLAY RIGHT OFF THE LINE! BUT... WAIT A SECOND...
TWEET!
THE REFS ARE CALLING A MAJOR PENALTY ON THRILLA!
SHE'S GOING TO THE PENALTY BOX!
THIS GIVES THE COLD ONES JUST THE OPPORTUNITY THEY NEED! SLAY IS THE LONE JAMMER OUT THERE— SO SHE IS THE ONLY ONE SCORING POINTS! THE COLD ONES CAN TURN THIS GAME AROUND!
AND SHE'S THROUGH THE PACK ONCE. REMEMBER, SHE WON'T START SCORING POINTS UNTIL HER NEXT TIME THROUGH THE PACK. SHE'S HEADING AROUND TURN TWO...

...SHE'S AT THE BACK OF THE PACK, IN SCORING POSITION!
OK, COLD ONES! HIT SOMEONE! GET ZOEY THROUGH THE PACK! GET HER THOSE POINTS, AND WE WIN THIS GAME!
HIT SOMEONE, ASTEROID!
HIT SOMEONE, ASTEROID!
THE COLD ONES ARE TRYING TO HELP SLAY MISERABLES... BUT SHE IS STUCK AT THE BACK OF THE PACK BEHIND BRAIDY PUNCH!
246 Slay Miserables
66 Braidy Punch
THAT BRAIDY PUNCH IS ONE SERIOUS BLOCKER—SHE IS NOT LETTING SLAY MISERABLES GET BY!

HELP!
ONLY 20 SECONDS LEFT ON THE CLOCK, AND SLAY IS **STILL** STUCK BEHIND BRAIDY PUNCH! IF SLAY DOES NOT GET PAST... THE BLACK DEATH WINS THIS GAME!
SUDDENLY, I KNEW WHAT I HAD TO DO.
HEY, BRAIDY! THERE'S ONLY ROOM FOR ONE BLUE-BRAIDED PLAYER ON THIS TRACK!
WAR FACE!
AAAAAAAGH!
Asteroid 12

SLAM!
PLINK
YOU CALL THAT A HIT, PIPSQUEAK?
OH NO.
AAAAAAAAGH!
OOOOHHHH! AND A **MASSIVE** HIT TO ASTEROID! BRAIDY PUNCH JUST LAUNCHED HER **WAY** INTO ORBIT!

AND YET, FROM MY VIEWPOINT IN THE AIR, I SAW IT...
BUT WAIT! LADIES AND GENTLEMEN! IN THAT ONE MOMENT OF DISTRACTION FOR BRAIDY PUNCH, SLAY MISERABLES GETS AROUND HER!
SHE GETS PAST BALD TO THE BONE! PAST MARZ ROLLVER!
ONE MORE SKATER TO GET PAST AND...
SHE DOES IT!
SLAY CALLS OFF THE JAM, AND THE COLD ONES WIN! FINAL SCORE, COLD ONES, 86, BLACK DEATH, 85!
OOOF!

I WATCHED MY TEAM RUSH OVER TO ZOEY, HUGGING AND YELLING...
... AND THEN I WATCHED ZOEY RUSH OVER TO ME.
ARE YOU OK?
MY ANKLE FEELS A LITTLE FUNNY... BUT I THINK I'M OK.
SEE, HEIDI? I DID LEARN SOMETHING, I—
YOU FELL SMALL, I KNOW. IF YOU DIDN'T GIVE ME ONE HEART ATTACK A DAY I'D THINK SOMETHING WAS WRONG. CAN YOU STAND UP?
I THINK SO.
ZOEY, HELP HER OVER TO THE MEDIC'S BENCH, WILL YOU?
LADIES AND GENTLEMEN...
... LET'S HEAR IT FOR ASTEROID!
THESE GIRLS ARE YOUNG, BUT THEY ARE JUST AS TOUGH AS ANY SKATER OUT THERE!
WOOO!
YEAH!

THE SECOND HALF OF THE ADULT BOUT STARTED THEN. ZOEY SAT WITH ME WHILE THE MEDICS LOOKED ME OVER.
OUCH!
MOM SAT WITH ME, TOO...
...OF COURSE.
MY BABY! MY SWEET BABY!
MOM! I'M FINE! I FEEL BETTER ALREADY.
IT LOOKS LIKE A MINOR SPRAIN. I WANT YOU TO SIT HERE AND KEEP THIS ICE ON YOUR ANKLE, OK?
OK.
WE WATCHED THE SECOND HALF OF THE GROWN-UP BOUT FROM THE SIDELINES. BEST SEATS IN THE HOUSE!
GO RAINBOW BITE!
MAN, DID YOU **SEE** THAT?
THAT WAS **SO** AWESOME—I WANT TO LEARN HOW TO DO THAT!

LADIES AND GENTLEMEN, RAINBOW BITE CALLS OFF THE JAM, MAKING THE FINAL SCORE PORTLAND 204, SEATTLE 117!
WHOOO!
YEAH, RAINBOW!
AND PORTLAND TAKES TO THE TRACK TO DO THEIR VICTORY LAP!
ROSEBUDS! HEY, ROSEBUDS! COME JOIN US ON OUR VICTORY LAP!
HOP

AFTER THE VICTORY LAP, I MET UP WITH MY TEAM.
THAT WAS **AMAZING**, ASTEROID!
I'VE NEVER SEEN ANYONE GET HIT SO HARD!
HEY PIPSQUEAK... I'M GLAD YOU'RE OK.
OW!
SLAY... COULD WE GET YOUR AUTOGRAPH?
OH... YEAH! SURE!
EXCUSE ME, ASTEROID?

WOULD YOU MIND SIGNING MY GRANDDAUGHTER'S PROGRAM?
MR. RANDOLPH? FROM THE EZ-STOP?
I SAW YOUR FLYER EVERY DAY IN THE STORE, AND I HAD TO SEE WHAT ALL THIS ROLLER SKATING WAS ABOUT! BESIDES, I THOUGHT YOU'D BE A GOOD ROLE MODEL FOR EMMY HERE.
I CAN ROLLER SKATE!
REALLY? DO YOU WANT TO PLAY ROLLER DERBY TOO?
YES!
ROLLER DERBY
WELL, IT'S A LOT OF HARD WORK... BUT IT'S REALLY FUN.
WHAT DO YOU SAY, EMMY?
ROLLER DERBY
THANK YOU!
AND THEN, THROUGH THE CROWD...
...I SAW HER.
Rollers

ARE YOU OK? I WANTED TO COME CHECK ON YOU, BUT MY DAD SAID NO.
I'M FINE. SEE? I CAN ALMOST PUT ALL MY WEIGHT ON IT.
NICE SOCKS!
THANKS.
HI, MR. B. HI, ADAM.
DUDE! THAT PART WHEN YOU WERE FLYING THROUGH THE AIR? I THOUGHT YOU TOTALLY BROKE YOUR BACK...
...THAT WAS AWESOME!
SOO... RACHEL DIDN'T COME?
NO, SHE...SHE COULDN'T MAKE IT. BUT ADAM WANTED TO COME, SO...
AND...IT SEEMS STUPID NOW, BUT... HERE. I BROUGHT YOU THESE.
NO, I... I LIKE THEM!

SO... I THINK WE'RE GOING TO GO. DO YOU WANT TO COME TO DINNER WITH US?
NICOLE HAS BEEN MY BEST FRIEND MY ENTIRE LIFE. FOR AS LONG AS I COULD REMEMBER, WE DID EVERYTHING TOGETHER.
AND YET...
I THINK...
I THINK I WANT TO STAY HERE.
WITH MY TEAM.
OH.
OK.
BYE, NICOLE.
YEAH. BYE, ASTRID.

IT'S FUNNY, HOW MUCH HAS CHANGED THIS SUMMER.
EVERYTHING USED TO BE SO SIMPLE. BLACK AND WHITE. HAPPY. SAD. BEST FRIENDS. WORST ENEMIES.
NOW EVERYTHING SEEMED SO... COMPLEX. I WAS IN A NO-MAN'S-LAND OF UNCHARTERED TERRITORIES.
MAYBE I HAD TO FIND MY OWN PATH THROUGH IT.
SUDDENLY, I LOOKED AT THE CROWD AROUND ME AND FELT... LOST. IT SOUNDS BABYISH, BUT I GOT A LITTLE PANICKED.
MOM? ZOEY?
THEY WERE HERE JUST A MINUTE AGO...
GASP!

THIS WAS MY CHANCE TO TALK TO HER IN PERSON. I **HAD** TO DO THIS. TOUGHER. STRONGER. FEARLESS.
EXCUSE ME, RAINBOW BITE?
"IT'S ME! ROSE DUD! YOUR BIGGEST FAN, YOUR SECRET PEN PAL..."
UM... COULD I PLEASE HAVE YOUR AUTOGRAPH?
ONE STEP AT A TIME.
SURE! ... IF I CAN HAVE YOURS!
ME?
YOU! THAT WAS SOME WICKED OFFENSE YOU WERE PLAYING. AND NEXT TIME, IF YOU ACTUALLY HIT THE GIRL OUT, YOU'LL BE EVEN BETTER!

OK!
I WAS REALLY STARTING TO PERFECT MY NEW SIGNATURE.
Asteroid
I HAVE TO TAKE OFF. YOU TAKE CARE OF THAT ANKLE OF YOURS, OK?
OK!
I QUICKLY FLIPPED TO WHERE SHE HAD SIGNED MY PROGRAM.
It takes a real hero to take a hit for the team, and to let the spotlight shine on someone else. Thanks for inspiring me. Your fan, Rainbow Bite
I ALMOST MISSED THE LAST PART:
P.S. "Asteroid" is a much better name than "Rose Dud."
WINK

WELL? ARE YOU COMING TO DINNER WITH US, OR WHAT? WE ALREADY ASKED YOUR MOM, SHE SAID IT'S ALL RIGHT.
WHAT? OH, UM, YEAH! SURE! LET ME JUST GRAB MY STUFF!
SLIDE

AND, THAT'S IT! THAT'S MY STORY OF ROLLER DERBY FAME...

. . . UNTIL THE NEXT BOUT,
OF COURSE.